A Place to Hide
Misty Hollow

Cynthia Hickey

ACKNOWLEDGMENTS

To those in love with Misty Hollow.

Chapter One

The sight of the pink envelope on her desk caused Marley Brooks's steps to falter. After two weeks of not receiving one, she'd thought her "fan" had moved on to harassing someone else. Despite being careful as she set her cup of coffee on her desk blotter, her hand trembled. Dark spots marred the white of the paper.

"Something wrong?" Her co-anchor at the local news station, Stan Blake, glanced up from his desk.

Marley forced a smile. "Lots of mail today."

"Oh. I almost forgot. Here's some mail that was set on my desk instead of yours." He smiled and handed her a stack of pink envelopes. "New mail clerk, I guess."

Her heart dropped to her knees. Hand shaking, she took the letters to her desk. They hadn't stopped after all. At first, the fan mail had started out nice, almost sweet, but as time went on, they'd taken on a menacing tone.

After glancing at the postmarks, she put them in order and opened the first one.

Marley!
I thought we were becoming friends. I mean, I

watch every. Single. Newscast. You're on. I still think you'd do better on the screen rather than in the field. You're easily the best there is. I've told you several times that all you have to do is say the word, and I'll clear the path for you. Get rid of the obstacles. For you, I'd do anything!

Your best friend.

The *do anything* remark chilled her blood. What exactly did the writer mean by that? She set the letter down and picked up the next one.

Marley,
Your nonresponse to my letters is beginning to be irksome. Yes, I said irksome. I'm an old-fashioned gal and like the sound of the old words. Did you miss my letter asking that you do a news report on the local animal shelter? How they're mistreating the animals? Or what about the soup kitchen? The food there is slop. I ought to know because I eat there on a regular basis. I save what little income I have for postage!

Really, if we're going to remain friends, you need to do some of the things I ask. That's what friends do. Remember, pretty is as pretty does, and you ignoring me is NOT PRETTY!

Your best friend (I think).

But Marley had visited both those places, and both seemed legit. She hadn't seen anything going on that warranted drawing the public's attention. She took a sip of her tepid coffee and thought about the people she'd seen at both places. Someone who had been at both.

Being a reporter gave her a good eye for details.

Who had stood out? Maybe someone overly friendly toward her? While she'd suspected her "fan" to be female, the last letter pretty much confirmed it. A man wouldn't call himself a gal.

With a sigh, she set down her cup and picked up the next letter. The postmarks were closer together. No longer one a week but several. Each letter more threatening. She opened the last one.

OK. We are obviously not friends. If we are not friends, we are enemies. I have wasted so much of my time writing to you, spilling out my feelings, trying to help you grow in your career. Why? Because I felt a connection the first time I saw you on TV.

Foolish me. Stupid Annie!

Tell Stan the Snake to watch his back. I'm going to use him as an example then...

I'M COMING FOR YOU!

Marley gasped.

"Something wrong?" Stan glanced up from his computer.

She bolted to her feet and dropped the letter on his desk.

He scanned the printed words. "Just a weirdo. Nothing to worry about."

"You think so?" She didn't. The writer was insane. "I think you should be worried. I am. We work together, Stan."

"Nah." He waved a dismissive hand. "It isn't the first time a crazy person has threatened me. They're all talk." He pushed to his feet. "I'm going to go grab me a breakfast sandwich from the coffee shop. Want anything?"

"No, thanks." She returned to her desk and stared at the pile of letters. They needed to be brought to the boss's attention and the police. "I'm going to show these to Merle. I should have as soon as they turned threatening."

"Suit yourself." He flashed his megawatt smile that had every female viewer's heart aflutter and sauntered out the door.

Could he be right? Was the writer nothing more than someone wanting attention and not to be worried about? No, she should err on the side of caution and show Merle.

She gathered up the letters, glancing outside before leaving the room. A crowd had gathered on the sidewalk waiting for the next bus.

Stan stood a few inches taller than most who waited, a big grin on his face as he bent to talk to a dark-haired woman. He waved and said something to someone else, then turned toward the street.

A scream rang out as he fell.

The city bus couldn't stop in time.

Stan's body hit the front of the bus, sending him flying.

The letters in Marley's hands fluttered to the floor like oversized rose petals. She sprinted from the building and outside as the crowd now circled Stan who lay on the road like a broken doll.

"A woman pushed him!" An elderly man leaning on a cane pointed down the street. "A woman with a knit cap on her head. I saw it as plain as day."

The fan meant every word she'd said. Marley needed to leave, find a place to hide. She darted back into the building and gathered up the letters before rushing to Merle's office. She quickly explained about Stan lying outside, the letters, and her taking a leave immediately. "I'll go by the police station, but I'm out of here for a while."

He stared at her as if she babbled in a language he didn't understand. "Stan was hit by a bus?"

"Yes." She shook her head. "I have to go. Please, go outside." Her throat clogged as she scooped up the letters. "I can't. I'll be in the open." She rushed to her office and grabbed her purse before ducking out the back door.

With every step toward the parking garage, she felt as if hands would press against her back and shove her in front of a moving vehicle. Inside her car, she locked the doors and sped from the garage toward the police station. If Annie followed her, maybe she'd lose her at the station.

The officer behind a desk frowned. "You've been receiving these for how long?"

"A few months." Her shoulders sagged.

"You didn't think anything of them?" He tilted his head.

"No." She sighed. "I'm going to take a leave for a while. Here is my cell phone number. Please call me if you find out anything."

He nodded, taking the business card from her hand. "I doubt we will. With you gone, this woman will probably find someone else to torment."

"She killed someone."

"Allegedly. We will treat this as an accident unless further evidence presents itself. Be careful, Miss Brooks. Any idea of where you're going?"

"No. I'm going to look for some rentals in the northern part of the state and go from there. Thank you." Outside, she glanced both ways before almost running to her car. Soon, she locked her apartment door behind her and tried to decide what to take since she had no idea how long she'd be gone.

Springtime weather didn't warrant warm clothes, so her suitcase could carry more. She filled the hard-sided case with clothes, toiletries, and the nine-millimeter Luger she'd only shot for target practice.

Packed, she logged onto her laptop and spent half an hour finding a place to rent for a while in a town called Misty Hollow deep in the mountains, then put the laptop into its bag, threw food and water into a box, and rushed back to her car several times to fit it all in. Ridiculous, really, but she didn't make enough money to repurchase everything.

With each trip she felt sharp eyes on her but didn't spot anyone. Not even a neighbor, but of course they were all still at work. Her breath came in gasps as she fought off a full-fledged panic attack, something she hadn't experienced in years.

Not now, please. After shoving the last item in the backseat of her car, she slid into the driver's seat. Her hands shook as she tried inserting the key into the ignition. Finally, she turned the key and the engine roared to life.

Should she stop at the bank? She definitely needed to fill up with gas. Every stop she needed to make could mean that Annie would find her. She'd gas up in a different town. No need to go to the bank. A homeless woman wouldn't know how to follow any withdrawals Marley might make.

Four and a half hours later, she drove down a winding mountain road into a picturesque town in a hollow. She continued following the GPS until she pulled in front of a lovely Victorian home. Wow. She couldn't believe the house could possibly rent for the amount she'd been given.

She exited the vehicle and hurried up the flagstone pathway to the porch. Before she climbed the stairs, a dark-haired woman with a baby on her hip opened the door.

"You must be Marley. I'm Gemma. Please come in." She stepped aside.

Marley stepped into luxury. "Wow."

"Yeah, my ex really did the place up. It's not exactly my taste, but we're headed to Europe for a while so there's no time to renovate. It's fully furnished."

"So much space for one person." She ran her hand over the polished banister of the sweeping staircase.

Gemma laughed. "Too much room for three, in my opinion, but we hope to fill the rooms with children. I'm sure you'll be happy here, Miss Brooks."

"You recognized me?"

"Of course. Your face is on the news every night. Don't worry. Folks around here mind their own business."

She'd hoped to be incognito longer. "How long do I have here?"

"At least six months."

Perfect. Marley faced the woman and thrust out her hand. "I'll take it. Six months is a perfect amount of time for a sabbatical."

Gemma returned the handshake. "Wonderful. I

need to run, so just drop the rental check off at the bank. Welcome to Misty Hollow. You'll love it here."

Marley followed the woman outside and stared up and down the street. Folks smiled and waved at the woman and child, several of them turning curious eyes on Marley. No one seemed to recognize her or, if they did, they chose not to say so.

She took a deep breath of the clean mountain air. Yes, she could be very happy here if no one showed up named Annie, or if she didn't receive any more "fan" letters.

No one could find her here.

Chapter Two

Gone? She'd fled and left her behind? Unacceptable. Especially after the way she'd poured her heart and soul into every letter she wrote to the ungrateful reporter.

Annie strolled out of tent city toward the nearest fast-food restaurant in order to charge her cell phone. The phone was her only expense other than a little food each day and the stationery and postage she needed to communicate with Marley. Her measly disability check didn't stretch far. Living in a cardboard palace helped, though.

She smiled as she sat at a table in the restaurant, ordered a breakfast sandwich, and plugged in her phone. Her palace really was nice in comparison. With duct tape in a bright pretty-pink shade, she'd taped together several appliance boxes. Oh, it had taken some time, but it was so worth it.

Inside, she'd found a scrap of carpet in a dumpster, some throw pillows she'd stitched up after finding them in someone's trash, an air mattress, blankets, even curtains from discarded fabric. Not that she let many people visit, but when they did, they were in awe of her creativity.

The first time she'd spotted Marley Brooks had been in front of a robbed convenience store. She'd reminded Annie so much of her Lauren who had drowned in the lake at the age of twelve. So, Annie had started corresponding with the reporter. Not that she expected any response, at first anyway. But her later letters had left the return address of the little old woman on Second Street who let Annie use her address for mail.

So, why no answer?

She turned on her phone and flipped through the icons until she found the tracking one. She held the screen closer to her eyes. "Misty Hollow? Why in the heck would she go there?" Having done her research, Annie knew Marley had no family to speak of. She'd been raised in the foster-care system. So why had she gone to a town in the mountains?

If she thought Annie couldn't find her, then Marley was the crazy one here.

~

Dirk Mason hefted a bag of seed onto his shoulder and turned from his truck. "Come on, Bear." His mastiff-German shepherd mix thumped his tail on the sidewalk.

"Hey!" A blond woman glared up at him. "You almost hit me with that." Shaking her head, she pushed past him, tossing her long hair over her shoulder.

Was that Marley Brooks? Here? He'd seen a few of her newscasts, but seeing the real person in Misty

Hollow was a bit of a shock. Had something happened in town that he didn't know about?

Dirk wrenched his gaze from her slim back and carried the seed into the mercantile. He'd ordered more than he needed, and his money would be better spent in repairing his broken tractor.

"Hey, Hank."

"Dirk." The hefty man leaned on his counter. "You know I can only give you store credit for returned seed."

"I know. I need some things for the tractor." He dropped the bag of seed and handed Hank the list. "I'll pay cash for the overage."

"How is the rice business?" Hank started pulling tractor parts off a shelf.

"Good when there's plenty of rain." Which they hadn't had that summer. Add in the fact that the family home he'd inherited from his grandparents needed some major work, and his money sometimes didn't stretch far enough. Thank God for his military pension.

"I'll come pick up my things after I grab a bite to eat at the diner. I have some other stops to make as well."

He entered the barber shop, Bear on his heels, and took a seat in the chair. "Just a trim, Barney."

"Same as always? Why not let your hair grow? You aren't in the army anymore."

"No fuss this way." He stared in the mirror at the barber. "Is that news reporter, Marley Brooks, doing a story in Misty Hollow?"

"Not that I know of. Rumor is she's taking a sabbatical."

Dirk's brows rose. Maybe reporting was a high-stress job. "I doubt she'll find much to do to pass the time here."

"If all she wants is rest, that's what she'll get." Barney turned on the shears, stopping the conversation.

Dirk didn't know why he cared about the reporter being here. Unless a person enjoyed hunting, fishing, hiking, or kayaking, there wasn't a lot to do in Misty Hollow. Sure, the place was beautiful, but Marley Brooks didn't strike him as the outdoorsy type. But, he'd been wrong before.

"Want me to pick you up a sandwich?"

Barney shook his head, brushing the loose hair from Dirk's shoulders. "Wife sent me with leftover pizza. I'm good. Tell Lucy and the chef I said hello."

"Will do." Dirk stood, handed the man a twenty-dollar bill, and left the shop. He ought to do his own hair and save the twenty bucks. Same as eating at the diner whenever he came to town.

"Stay." He motioned for Bear to lie down in a patch of grass outside Lucy's diner. "I'll bring you a big, juicy burger."

The dog wagged his tail and laid his chin on folded paws.

~

"Whoa." Marley jumped back at the sight of the massive black and brown dog taking residence near the diner. "Are you friendly?"

The dog's tail thumped the grass.

She sure hoped so. Marley gave the dog's head a pat on her way past and burst through the front doors as if the hounds of hell were nipping at her heels.

Heads turned. One handsome man in a blue and black flannel shirt that he'd cut the sleeves off of smiled.

Not wanting to encourage anyone's conversation, she asked for a table in the back. The hostess led her to a booth in a far corner near the hall leading to the restrooms and right next to Mr. Flannel before handing her a menu.

"Welcome to Misty Hollow. Your server will be with you shortly." The red-haired woman headed for the kitchen.

"Lucy." The flannel-wearing man waved her over. "You didn't tell me the special."

"Sorry, Dirk. It's chicken fried chicken, mashed potatoes, and green beans."

"I'll take it."

Sounded good, but Marley's career depended on her looking a certain way. When her server took her order, she asked for soup and a salad.

Mr. Flannel folded his hands on the table in front of him and stared out the window.

Marley tore her gaze away. She was here to stay to herself until the crazed fan moved on to someone else. A few months to get rid of the fear hanging over her like a cloud ready to burst. While she waited, she'd get the rest she sorely needed and start writing the true-crime book she'd always wanted to write. The six months would fly by.

She pulled a pad of paper and a pen from her purse. While she ate, she could take notes for the book. Better than sitting there alone staring at the handsome man in flannel who kept glancing her way. If she looked busy, maybe he'd transfer his attention back outside.

"Here you go." The red-haired Lucy set her order

in front of her. "I didn't have time to introduce myself, but I'm the owner of this diner, Lucy Romano."

"Marley Brooks."

"Oh, dear, we all know who you are. There's no better place for a sabbatical than Misty Hollow. Although—" she arched a brow, "there's usually trouble when a pretty woman arrives here alone." She grinned and moved to the kitchen.

Marley stared after her. What kind of trouble? She glanced wide-eyed at Mr. Flannel. Did the men here bother new women? At the first sign of such behavior, she'd pack up and move, breaking her six-month lease. She had enough trouble without men harassing her.

The French onion soup was the best she'd ever had. Good enough for any fine-dining restaurant. She glanced through the kitchen window at the chef. He looked familiar. Ah. She recognized the highly sought-after chef who had chosen small-town life. While she couldn't remember his name, she never forgot a face.

She narrowed her eyes when she caught Mr. Flannel staring her way again. The man didn't seem flirtatious; in fact, his stern gaze was unnerving. Why was he so interested in her?

She flagged down her server. "Who is that man?"

"That's Dirk Mason. Isn't he dreamy? But, he's a bit of a loner. Has been for a long time. I heard it's because a woman left him at the altar."

"It's true what they say about small towns. Everyone knows everything about everyone. Thank you." She wouldn't pry. Most people had heartaches they wanted to keep hidden. The town most likely wouldn't let poor Mr. Mason forget about his broken heart.

No wonder he seemed to glare her way. He probably blamed all women for the betrayal. She smiled his way, not receiving one in return, and transferred her attention back to her notes.

A man with a star pinned to his navy-blue shirt entered the diner, glanced around, and then headed in Marley's direction. "Miss Brooks, I'm Sheriff Westbrook. I contacted the police department in Little Rock. Seems you've had a bit of trouble, and that's what brought you here."

"Do you check out every newcomer to town?" She tilted her head.

"We've had some issues lately, so yes. I now check out every new resident. How long are you staying?"

"I signed a six-month lease."

"That didn't answer my question, but I'll let it slide. I want to know immediately if you receive another fan letter."

"Why would I? The person writing those letters can't possibly know where I've gone."

"Ma'am, if there's one thing I've learned in my career in FBI and as sheriff, there is always a way for someone who's determined."

Chapter Three

Whatever the sheriff said seemed to really upset the news reporter. She paled to the color of parchment paper.

Dirk stopped the sheriff as he passed his table. "Is everything okay?"

"Sure hope so." He cleared his throat. "Keep an eye out for other strangers in town, will you? I could be overly cautious, but it's better than not cautious at all."

"Sure." *That question was as vague as they come.* "She in trouble?"

"Possibly. Just keep your eyes open for me, will you? Have a good day, Dirk." The sheriff clapped him on the shoulder and left the diner.

Dirk's gaze shifted to Miss Brooks. Her wide eyes darted from him to the sheriff and back to him. What could possibly be going through that blond head of hers?

She waved the server over. A few seconds later, she headed for the cashier, then outside.

Dirk paid his ticket and followed. "Come, Bear." His dog padded alongside him as they followed the woman to the bank. Trying to be as inconspicuous as possible, Dirk bought a newspaper from a machine outside the drugstore and pretended to read.

Marley exited the bank and, without looking in his direction, headed down the sidewalk to the corner store. Dirk again told Bear to stay and followed, grabbing a basket from a pile near the door. He could always use a few groceries. When Marley went to one lane to pay, he went to the other, then waited a few seconds before leaving the store. He didn't want to be too conspicuous.

He followed her to the library and sat on a bench near the duck pond. That seemed like a relatively normal thing to do. While he waited, he ran through his mind what he should be doing that day, and none of it included following a woman around town.

"Are you following me?"

He turned and stared into the irate face of Marley Brooks. She clutched three library books in her arms. "Uh…no?"

"Is that a question or an answer?"

Bear thumped his tail, drawing her attention to him.

"Is he friendly?"

"Absolutely. That's why I feel safe not having him on a leash." Dirk pushed to his feet. "I, uh, the sheriff asked me to help keep an eye on you because you might be in trouble."

Her eyebrows rose. "Really?" She sagged onto the bench. "He must think the trouble toward me will come here."

Dirk sat beside her as Bear gave a small whine and rested his big head on her knee. "Mind telling me what kind of trouble? I'll help if I can."

She patted his dog's head and glanced at him. "Why would you help me? You don't even know me."

"You're a fellow human being, aren't you?" He gave her a lopsided smile. "I have a soft spot for creatures in trouble. Found this big loot limping on the side of the road when he was about a year old. Took him in, and he's now my best friend. My name is Dirk Mason, by the way."

"Marley Brooks. A dog?"

"Sure, why not? Animals are a lot better than people in my opinion." He stared at the pond as a mallard and its family swam past. He wouldn't pressure her to tell him about her troubles, but if Westbrook wanted him to keep an eye on her, Dirk needed to know. One more thing to add to his increasing workload. How was he supposed to watch her and work the farm?

"I need to get back to my farm. Can I give you a ride somewhere? Maybe it isn't safe for you to be walking around."

"Unless I spot trouble, I'm fine. I seriously doubt my crazed fan will find me here."

So, she had a stalker. Dirk scanned those walking around the pond or fishing. No one seemed to pay them any attention. Maybe she was right, and she'd found a safe place in Misty Hollow. "Let me give you my number. Call me at any time if you need me."

"That's very kind of you." She typed his number into her phone as he recited it. "I'll send you a text so you can save my number. Thank you for caring." She retrieved her books from the bench and marched away.

"Nothing more we can do for her. Come on, Bear." Dirk made his way to the feed store and retrieved his purchases. On his way home, he passed Marley entering the big Victorian house bought by the ex-fiancé of a mob boss.

~

Annie packed up as many of her belongings as she could fit in a large box. She hated leaving behind her palace to stay in a tent again, but it couldn't be helped. Maybe, she could find a cheap motel room to rent while she connected with Marley.

If she found herself a job, even a measly minimum-wage job, she could afford a room. She sold her palace, at least the outer shell of it, to a fellow homeless woman for the cost of a bus ticket. If she returned here, she could always build herself another cardboard home.

Rather than use the money for a ticket, she dragged her box of things to the Interstate and flagged down a semi-truck. "Take me as close to Misty Hollow as you can."

"To where?" The man frowned.

"Here." She pulled up a map on her phone. "As far as you can. I'll find a way to continue." Hitchhiking was her major mode of transportation. No one suspected a homeless woman capable of harm, and she didn't mind riding in the back of trucks to get where she needed to go.

"Okey doke."

Four hours later, he dropped her in a town she hadn't caught the name of. "Good luck, lady." After Annie retrieved her box, she dragged it toward the bus station.

"How much for a ticket to Misty Hollow?"

"No bus to Misty Hollow. You'll have to hire a

ride or beg for one." The ticket master didn't even look up.

"Any ideas of who would be kind enough to take me there? How far is it?"

"About forty miles. Takes thirty minutes if you drive fast." He glanced up, his eyes narrowing. "We don't want no homeless riffraff around here."

"Good thing I'm moving on then, isn't it? Do you know of someone or not?"

"Not."

Annie muttered a curse and left the building. On the sidewalk, she peered up and down the street. Maybe if she cleaned up, put on some presentable clothes, she could find someone kind enough to give her a ride. A shower would go a long way to making her acceptable.

Using some of her precious-few dollars, she rented a motel room for the night and showered, her mind trying to come up with a way to complete her journey.

The next morning, dressed in clean clothes with freshly shampooed hair, she stepped into a small diner. "Anyone here headed to Misty Hollow and willing to give me a ride?"

"I will. I'm making a delivery. Come share a meal with me." A man around sixty-years-old waved over a server. "Put her meal on my bill."

"That's very kind of you." Annie took a seat across from him and ordered the breakfast special. It would be enough to take leftovers with her. "I'm Annie."

"Steve. Why are you needing a ride?"

"I'm running from an abusive boyfriend." She forced a smile. "Figured a remote place in the mountains would work as a good place to hide."

"Lots of folks try, but Misty Hollow is starting to

gain a reputation as a place for people to retreat. There are lots of folks vacationing and camping around those parts now. Not as remote as it used to be."

"You live there?"

"Nah. Just make the occasional delivery of lumber."

After she ate and had the server box up her leftovers, Annie climbed into the front seat of a truck pulling a trailer of cut lumber. "I appreciate it."

"Not a problem. Won't be able to take you down Main Street. I'm not allowed with this load."

"A motel would be great."

"There's one right on the outskirts of the town."

Steve dropped her in the motel parking lot. "Good luck, Annie."

She nodded and shoved her box into the motel lobby. A help-wanted sign hung in the window. Things were falling right into place for her.

"I need a room and the job."

"It's cleaning rooms. Gives you minimum wage and a room with a kitchenette if you need a place to stay. You get paid every Friday, which means you'll earn two days' pay this week if you start in the morning."

"Sounds perfect."

"Fill out these papers, and the job is yours," the manager said. "I'm Rob Jones. This job has been available for quite a while. I'm glad to have you. What brings you to Misty Hollow?"

"I'm looking for a friend and a new start."

Half an hour later, Annie put her things away in a room with a full bathroom, a dinette, a bed, sleeper sofa, and a table with two chairs. The best part was the room didn't cost her anything but her time. Once everything was in its place, she locked the room and walked to a convenience store on the corner to purchase some necessities and food.

She wanted to ask the clerk if he knew where Marley Brooks was staying. Her tracker didn't pinpoint the exact location, only the area, but that might raise some red flags. Annie would have to be patient. It was a small town after all.

~

Marley double-checked all the doors and windows to make sure they were locked—even the ones on the second floor.

The fact that the sheriff asked Dirk to watch over her left her chilled. He must truly believe that Annie would find her. How? She'd told no one but the police of her destination.

She gasped. Did Annie work for the police department? No. What a ridiculous idea.

She plopped on the sofa and turned on the television that took up most of one wall. Scanning the channels, she stopped at the news station she worked for.

One of the night anchors spoke about Stan's death which had been ruled a homicide. Several witnesses had seen him pushed by a woman, but no one could give a good description of her. The police were asking for anyone who could help to give them a call. Thank goodness there was no mention of Marley leaving, which she preferred. Eventually, people would wonder where she was. The answer of her taking a sabbatical would satisfy curiosity.

She turned off the TV. Would she be safe here?

She glanced around the room. No one would break into the house. The previous owner had installed so much security it was like Fort Knox.

No, if Annie came for Marley, it would be outside. On the street or while shopping. She shuddered. Maybe there truly was nowhere safe for a person to hide. Maybe the sheriff was right, and a person could always be found.

Loneliness poured over her like a waterfall. One that fell with such force it threatened to send her to her knees. She had no one to confide her fears in. No one she could trust. If Annie came to Misty Hollow, an innocent comment could tell her where Marley was.

How was she going to keep herself safe?

Chapter Three

After work, Annie headed to the diner where anyone could find out anything. According to her boss, the diner was the town's gossip den, its gathering place. While she hated using her spare funds, she could at least get coffee and a slice of pie while asking questions.

Wouldn't it be wonderful if she actually ran into Marley? Annie could introduce herself as Jane, her mother's middle name. Marley would be none the wiser. Of course, it might be a smarter thing simply to observe at first.

The thought put a spring in her step as she practically skipped to Lucy's Diner. A bell jingled over her head as she entered. A few heads glanced her way, but since Annie wasn't one to attract much attention, being plain and modestly dressed, their gazes didn't linger. She enjoyed being invisible.

She took a seat at the counter and ordered coffee and possum pie. Why not indulge in chocolate heaven? She was about to make friends with her idol. Annie glanced around the diner. No sign of the woman she sought. Ah, there she was coming out of the ladies room. Annie ducked her head as Marley passed on her way out the door.

When she'd gone, she summoned the server's attention. "Was that Marley Brooks, the news reporter?"

"Yep." The woman grinned. "She's renting the big Victorian on Oak Street. Fancy digs. No idea why a woman alone would want such a large place." She shrugged. "The price must be right. Anyway, it's nice having a celebrity in our midst. Of course, none of us treat her any differently. Everyone is the same in Misty Hollow." She refilled Annie's coffee and moved to the next customer.

Annie forked a giant bite of chocolate goodness into her mouth. Good. She wouldn't have any trouble finding out where Marley lived. Quickly finishing her treat, she laid money on the counter, and returned to her room.

~

If Marley planned on writing her true crime series, she'd need a planner for plotting on paper, her preference. She'd searched the Victorian for a notebook but found nothing. So, hoisting her purse over her shoulder, she stepped onto her porch the next morning prepared to head to either a supermarket or a bookstore, whichever came first.

A paper fluttered, catching her eye. She gasped. Her hand trembled as she reached for the note taped to her front door.

Hello, Marley,
You're looking very good. What a beautiful place

you've found. If you need a roommate, let me know. That's an awful big place for you to live in all by yourself.

Aren't you giddy with excitement that I'm here? We can really get to know each other now.

Annie

P.S. Sorry about Stan.

Sorry about Stan? The woman had killed him in order to get Marley's attention. That couldn't be forgiven.

Marley lowered to the top step. How had this woman found her? A bug on her car? Her phone? Maybe her first stop for the day should be the mechanic's shop. Her heart might threaten to beat out of her chest, but Marley wouldn't hide. No, she'd move forward until the time came to confront this crazy fan of hers.

She dug in her bag for her cell phone. Once she had it in her grasp, she called Dirk. "I'm sorry, but you're the only one in town I know."

"It's not a problem. Are you okay?"

"I…received a note…on my door. From my stalker." She closed her eyes. She shouldn't have called him. No sense in getting him involved. "I'm sorry. I'll let you go."

"No. Wait. Go inside. I'll be there in fifteen minutes."

"Okay." She jumped to her feet and rushed into the house, slamming and locking the door behind her.

So, the woman had left a note on the door. It hadn't sounded threatening like the last ones. The woman couldn't get into the house. Not with its top-notch security. As long as Marley didn't go out alone at night, staying where there were people around when she did go out, she'd be fine. Once she found out how Annie tracked her down, everything would be fine.

Marley jumped when a knock sounded on the door. She peeked out the peephole, relieved to see Dirk. Had she really stood there lost in thought for fifteen minutes? She opened the door and ushered him in. "Thank you. I didn't know who else to call." From the dirt on the knees of his jeans, she'd interrupted work of some kind. "If you're busy—"

"I said everything was fine." He frowned. "Let me see the note. I'm former military PD, so I might be able to help you. That's why the sheriff asked me to watch over you. We don't exactly have a large sheriff's department here."

Retired military? Hope leaped in her heart. She handed him the note. "I think either my phone or my car is bugged. How could she follow me otherwise? I'm hoping you'll follow me to the mechanic."

"I'd be happy to." He led the way back outside, pausing on the porch while she locked up. "Drive straight down Main Street. You'll see Roy's Garage on your left. Do you mind if I look over your car first?"

"No." What did he expect to see? A tracker? A bomb? She put a hand over her mouth to stifle a gasp.

Dirk cut her a quick glance, then peered under the car. "Okay. You're good." He waited until she was in the car before climbing into his truck.

Ten minutes later, she pulled into the parking lot of the garage and slid out of her car as a man in dark coveralls strolled her way. He wiped his hands on a rag before offering to shake hers. "Welcome. I'm Roy." He looked past her. "You here with Dirk?"

"He followed me, yes. This might sound strange, but could you check to see whether there's a tracking device planted on my car?"

He laughed. "This is Misty Hollow. After the last year and a half, that is not a strange request at all. Sure. Hang out a bit. Won't take me long. Keys in the ignition?"

"Yes." She stepped back as he drove her car into one of the bays.

"Want to join me for breakfast while he looks over your car?" Dirk hung out his truck window. "Lucy makes great biscuits and gravy. You can even have chocolate gravy if you want."

She hadn't had that since she was little. "That sounds great." Marley rushed to the passenger side and climbed in. "I'd also like to buy a pretty notebook and pens."

"We can stop by the bookstore after breakfast. Not a problem."

At Lucy's she ordered chocolate gravy and biscuits. Dirk ordered a multi-meat omelet with hash browns and toast.

"What work did I interrupt when I called?" Lucy reached for her water glass.

"Trying to get my tractor running. It's old and cranky."

"You don't look old enough to be retired military."

"I'm not." He straightened against the back of the booth. "I spent ten years in, then when my father died, I inherited the farm. Figured I'd come home and see whether I could make a go of it."

From the shadow that passed across his features,

she guessed things weren't going as well as planned. "And I'm keeping you from reaching that goal."

"Stop apologizing. I told you to call if you needed me."

True, but she couldn't help feeling guilty by involving him.

After breakfast, Dirk paid the bill despite her protests. He then drove her to the bookstore. She headed straight to the stationery aisle and chose a beautiful floral notebook with matching ink pen and refills. The purchase should really inspire her to start her book.

"That's fancy."

"I'm writing a book. I want to plot it out using something pretty."

"A novel, huh?" He smiled.

"True crime. Based on some of the stories from the station." She placed her purchase on the floorboard of the truck. "Thanks again."

"Again, not a problem." He drove them back to the garage.

Roy met them next to her car. "Vehicle's clean. No tracking device. It's in good mechanical condition overall."

Then her cell phone. "Where can I get a new phone?"

"Hank's mercantile sells cell phones. They have several plans to choose from, or you can go to Langley."

"Hank's sounds fine." If she couldn't find the type of phone she was used to, she could always change once this Annie woman left her alone.

~

"I'll follow you." Since his day had already been interrupted, Dirk might as well continue until Marley was safely in her house.

"You don't have to."

"I insist."

She looked as if she regretted disrupting his day, then nodded. "See you there."

Hank's was two blocks over. Dirk found an empty spot several cars from the door. Marley had already stepped inside the store by the time he was out of his truck.

Yes, she'd interrupted a job he really needed to complete. Did he regret it? No. Not if it meant reassuring a woman in trouble that there was someone around who cared about her welfare. Someone willing to help her. The tractor wasn't going anywhere. It wasn't harvest season yet, so time wasn't too critical.

"You'll need to destroy your old phone, just to be safe." He joined Marley at the store counter where a box with a new phone sat.

Hank, the owner, gave him a strange look. "Sounds suspicious."

"Could be." Dirk smiled. "You know what happens whenever a pretty gal arrives in town alone."

He nodded. "Yep. Trouble."

Marley glanced from one to the other. "What does that mean?"

"You're a reporter." Dirk faced her. "You must know about all that's happened in this town over the last year or so. It's always after a new woman arrives in town."

Her eyes widened. "You can't possibly believe that has anything to do with the uprise in crime."

"Strange coincidences, then. Anyway, it's better to be safe by destroying the old phone."

She turned back to Hank. "Can you transfer all my files, apps, and contacts before I do that?"

"Sure can. Take a look around the store. This will take a bit."

The two of them strolled up and down aisles that carried a little bit of everything. The mercantile had always reminded Dirk of a general store from a hundred years ago. Back when the town was just getting started. He wouldn't be surprised if the mercantile had been around that long.

"Need anything?" He asked.

"Not really. The house I'm renting has everything a person could think of needing." She ran her hand over one of the throw pillows, and waved it back and forth, sending the sequins in a riot of color.

"This is relaxing." She grabbed the pillow. "Maybe I do need this."

He chuckled at the nonsense purchase. "It wouldn't hurt to put some personal touches in the place."

"I don't plan on staying longer than six months."

He'd known her fewer than twenty-four hours, yet knowing she'd be in Misty Hollow for such a short time left him with a feeling of sadness. Maybe he needed to get more involved around town, make some friends— not stay to himself so much.

In addition to the pillow, Marley ended up purchasing a coffee mug depicting her as an author, a tape dispenser in the shape of a stiletto, and a ceramic pencil holder covered in painted flowers. None of it went together, but together they provided a bit of color and whimsy.

"I know they don't make sense, but nothing in my life does right now. I might as well surround myself with things that make me smile." She set the items on the counter.

"I tore your old phone apart. Didn't find any physical bugs, but there are ways to track someone with an app. Even if they aren't aware. The new phone is ready."

Marley handed over a credit card. Outside, she put her purchases in the front passenger seat of her car. "Since the woman is already in town, buying a new phone won't keep her from finding me, but at least she won't know every move I make."

That might be the very thing that kept Marley from being harmed.

Chapter Five

Marley sat on the back deck, coffee in hand, notebook in her lap, and watched the sun rise over the trees behind the house. Since she'd woken up far too early that morning worrying about Annie, why not witness the birth of a new day? Hopefully, it would help inspire her to start writing and take her mind off her stalker.

Which of the past news stories should she focus on? She set down her cup and picked up her laptop, placing it in her lap. If she spent time skimming the database, something was bound to jump out at her.

As she searched, her mind switched gears. Rather than a true-crime story, she'd pick an unsolved crime and make it a fictional retelling with a satisfying ending. Her own brand of justice.

"Oh, this is good," she murmured. She'd found an unsolved crime eerily similar to her own circumstances. An author, rather than a news reporter, had received fan letters of an increasingly hostile nature. After similar months, the author had been found dead in her home from multiple stab wounds. The "fan" had never been caught. Police sent it to cold case last year.

She drummed her fingers on the arm of her wicker chair. If she took all the information in the files and added what was happening to her, even adding in Stan's death, she might have a bestseller on her hands. Marley knew firsthand the fear that would've rippled through the dead author. She could put emotion in the writing. Real emotion.

She sent the files to her printer via Wi-Fi and picked up her coffee cup, her gaze settling on the view again. A beautiful place. From the backyard, a person wouldn't know the front sat on a residential street. Lovely and lonely. How was she going to survive alone for six months? What if Annie wasn't found in that time? What if she came at Marley with a knife?

Maybe she needed to take a class on self-defense. Dirk could probably help with that since he used to be military.

After carrying her things into the house, she sent him a text. A call would only pull him from his work. This way, she hoped, he'd answer at his leisure.

The house was too quiet. She packed up the printed files and her laptop, slipping it all into a laptop backpack, and headed to the local coffee shop. She didn't want a lot of noise, but a bit in the background helped keep her grounded.

Marley shot constant glances over her shoulder as she made her way to the shop. She could've driven, but she lived so close to Main Street it seemed a waste of gas. If she stayed vigilant, only went out alone during the day, she'd be fine.

She chose a table in a corner of the coffee shop, plugged in her laptop, and then stepped up to the counter. Having studied the menu choices, she chose a bagel with cream cheese and a mocha-flavored, blended coffee.

"How are you liking it here?" The barista, a young woman in her early twenties, smiled. "I watched you on the news all the time. Did you quit?"

"No. I'm taking time off to write a book." Marley stifled a sigh. She might as well prepare herself to be asked that question many times over the next week or so. "I'll only be in town for six months."

"Well, we're happy to have you." She handed Marley her order.

"Thank you." Drink in hand, she headed for her table.

A woman strolled past, taking a quick glance at the papers Marley had left there, tossed a smile Marley's way, then continued to the ladies room. Marley sat at the table and booted up her laptop. Time to get started.

"Are you Marley Brooks?" The woman who had passed her table, stopped. "From the news?"

Marley pasted on a smile. "Yes."

"It's nice to meet you. I'm Jane. I work over at the Misty Motel. Not fancy, but it's a job. Well, I see you're busy. I'm around if you need a friend."

"Thank you, Jane." Marley kept the pleasant look on her face until the woman exited the shop, then returned to her work.

Her cell phone buzzed with a text from Dirk giving his address and saying he had some free time that afternoon. Wonderful. Time to learn how to defend herself.

~

What was she doing?! Annie marched around the

corner of the building and sagged against the warm brick. Why did Marley have the files on the murder of that author in full view of anyone passing by? She almost had a heart attack when she saw them.

Annie really didn't want a repeat of those events. Sharon Follett had never been receptive to Annie's gesture of friendship. For that she paid the ultimate price.

But Marley was special. She looked so much like what Annie had imagined Lauren would have, if she hadn't died at the age of twelve. Things would be different this time. She'd make sure.

~

Dirk tightened the bolt on the tractor tire and straightened, popping the kinks from his back. When he'd read Marley's text, it had pleased him that she wanted him to teach her self-defense. It wasn't the first time. He'd often taught classes while in the military. Sometimes, he thought about opening a place in Misty Hollow, but the farm took all his time.

It occurred to him on a regular basis that the only reason he had taken over the farm was out of obligation after his father died. Not because he shared his father's passion. He'd had an offer for the land, but couldn't bring himself to sell.

What he needed to do was find another use for the land, since farming wasn't his thing. A while back, he'd once considered running a tiny house community for homeless veterans.

He glanced around the land with a fresh eye. Why not? The residents could work the rice fields until something better came along. Or not. But, they could work instead of paying rent, and everyone would benefit. That would leave Dirk time to open a self-defense studio. He'd start making plans that very evening. For the first time since arriving back in Misty Hollow two years ago, he had hope for the future.

The crunch of tires on gravel pulled him out of the garage and to the front of the house. Marley parked next to his truck, then stepped onto his driveway, wearing leggings and a tank top—looking way too sexy in his opinion. The fact the woman didn't seem overly focused on her beauty made her all the more appealing.

"Thank you. I hope I'm not disturbing you."

"Your timing couldn't be more perfect. I just finished. Let me wash up. Meet me out back. I'll bring a wrestling mat."

Her eyes widened. "You plan on throwing me down?"

"Absolutely." He grinned and entered the house. Flipping a pretty lady over his shoulder was never an unpleasant experience. He looked forward to wrestling with Marley. No better way to spend his afternoon in his opinion.

He took a quick shower to wash off the grime and sweat, then pulled on a pair of jeans and a tee shirt before retrieving the mat from the closet under the stairs. He carried it outside and dropped it on the grass. "Want something to drink?"

"No, thanks. I brought something." She held up a cup with a lid and straw. "Is there anything I need to do?"

"Let me ask you some questions first." He motioned for her to have a seat on the deck steps. "Are you wanting only some physical tips, or do you want to learn to shoot? That is, assuming you don't know how."

"I don't know how. Do you think I should learn?" Her eyes widened.

"Considering you have a mad woman after you, yes." His heart skipped a beat when she told him the plot of the book she'd decided to write.

"Do you think it could be the same person?"

"I don't know, but it's eerily similar." He pushed to his feet. "I have a Ruger nine-millimeter I'll lend you until you buy one of your own."

She stood. "I guess that means I should learn."

"It wouldn't hurt for you to carry pepper spray either. Maybe a Taser."

She frowned. "I don't want to be weighed down like a police officer, Dirk. I'll go with the pepper spray when I can't take the gun. Deal?"

"Deal." He playfully thrust out his hand. Hers fit perfectly when she returned his shake.

Dirk showed her a move that had her flat on her back. He stared into eyes the color of a summer sky and lost his breath for a minute. Maybe this wasn't such a good idea.

She wrapped her legs around his waist, and before he knew what had happened, he was the one staring at the sky. "I saw that in a movie."

"Good move." He swallowed against a dry throat. If he was going to be any help to her, he'd need to remain professional. Hard to do with her looking down at him, pieces of her hair falling free of her ponytail and tickling his face.

"This is fun. Show me something else." She rolled off him and got to her feet, holding out her hand to help him up.

"Think you're hot stuff now because you put one

over on me?"

"Yep." Her eyes twinkled. "Show me what to do if someone comes up behind me. Then, if they come at me from the front."

He gladly obliged, even throwing in some karate kicks. "If you come here every day, I'm confident you'll be able to sufficiently defend yourself." Except from a bullet she didn't see. Short of wrapping her in Kevlar, he was doing the best he could.

"Let's take a break, then I'll set up some cans for you to use as targets." He went into the kitchen and returned with two glasses of iced tea. "Want sugar?"

"No. I'm one of those who doesn't care for sweet tea. Thanks." She clinked her glass against his. "For this and the training."

"Not a problem. It breaks up the monotony of my days." Realizing how pathetic that made him sound, he added, "This place keeps me busy, but it's still nice to do something different." Not much better. He raised his glass to his lips to keep from saying anything else stupid. He set the glass on the porch railing. "Sun's going down soon, and I don't want you arriving to a dark house. If we're going to shoot, we'd better get to it."

She glanced at the time on her phone. "Raincheck. You're right. I don't want it to be dark when I arrive home." Marley collected her things, thanked him again, and hurried to her car.

Loneliness assailed him again as she drove away. Bear, who had been gone for several hours in the woods, leaned against his leg. "You got a girlfriend out there, Bear? I missed you today." He scratched behind the dog's ears. "Maybe you could lend your sweetheart to Marley? A dog wouldn't be a bad thing to have if someone tried to harm her."

He wondered what the rental policy was where she lived. She might not even like dogs. But it wasn't his place to make decisions for her. If Marley wanted a dog, she'd buy one. Just like she'd taken the initiative to ask him to train her.

With one more glance at the road, he told himself to call her in a few minutes to make sure she made it home safely. It had been a long time since he'd had someone to worry about. He didn't know whether he wanted to shake the sheriff's hand or punch him.

Chapter Six

Annie glared at the enormous, leather-wearing man in front of her. "I'm not the manager."

"I asked for twenty rooms over a month ago." He slapped his hands on the counter. "I've got a bunch of motorcycle-riding friends arriving this afternoon. So…what are you going to do about it?"

It wasn't that they didn't have the rooms, they did. They also didn't take reservations, so she wasn't quite sure why Hamed would've told this man they did. "The manager isn't here right now."

The man growled. "Are the rooms available or not?"

"They are."

"Fine. I'll book them now for the next five days."

"Very well, sir. Are you having a rally of some sort?"

"Yes. Riding along the mountain roads has become an annual favorite." He straightened while she logged in to the computer.

Annie was the maid, not the manager. If Hamed was going to take this much time off, she should demand a raise. Now, she'd be rushing the next two hours to make sure the rooms were ready for check-in. She collected the room cards and handed them to Mr. Dave Wakes. "Enjoy your stay."

He shook his head, looking at her as if she were simpleminded. "*I'm* not staying here. I live in Misty Hollow." With one last exasperating glimpse her way, he stormed out the door.

Well, how was she supposed to know who lived here and who didn't? One look at the clock had her flipping the sign on the door to "Gone to Lunch" and rushing toward the diner. This was the time Marley usually showed up, and Annie didn't want to miss seeing her.

Her shoulders slumped as she stepped into the diner and didn't see the one she sought. They lifted again when Marley burst through the doors less than a minute after Annie. She smiled in her direction, then headed for a back booth.

Something seemed different about Marley. Annie narrowed her eyes. Confidence? When Annie had first arrived in Misty Hollow, there had been an air of what? Nervousness? Fear? Something that had started after she'd received Annie's letters. Now, Marley's head was high and her back straight. What had changed?

Rather than sit at the counter as she usually did, she slid into the booth in front of Marley. If she spoke to anyone, Annie would hear.

~

"Good morning." Lucy, order pad in hand, stopped at Marley's table. "Heard you've been spending a lot of time at Dirk's farm. Small town, you know?" She grinned.

Marley laughed. "I'm learning there are no secrets here. Yes, I spend a few hours each afternoon helping him with plans for a homeless community for veterans. He could use the help on the farm, so this would benefit far more people than just him."

"It would be nice to put a roof over the heads of some of those living out by the lake. Dirk is a good man. What can I bring you today?"

Marley cut a quick glance at the specials board. "Bacon avocado BLT with fries, please. Water is fine."

"Coming right up."

While she waited, Marley pulled her notebook from her bag. She'd managed to plot out the first couple of chapters but wanted at least five before she started writing. Since this was her first novel, six months might not be enough time. She'd have very little time to write once she returned to work.

Marley shifted her glaze toward the large front window of the diner. What if she didn't return to news work? She had a bit of savings. Maybe she could find a little place to call home in Misty Hollow. Give full-time writing a try. Maybe do some freelance work for the station until royalties started coming in. She smiled, liking the idea of no more big-city bustle. The idea warranted some deep thought.

"Hello." The woman she'd met at the coffee shop paused by her table. "Jane, remember?" She put a hand on her flannel shirt-covered chest.

"I do. How are you?" Marley closed her notebook.

"I'm good. Grabbing a quick lunch before returning to work." Her chest puffed out. "Acting manager for a week. Lots to do."

"At the Misty Motel, right?"

"You remembered!" Jane's smile widened.

"It's my job to remember details." Now if she'd just move on so Marley could get to plotting. She was due at Dirk's in an hour.

When Lucy arrived with her lunch, the woman continued to the restroom. Breathing a sigh of relief, Marley bit into her sandwich. The tangy creaminess of the avocado and the saltiness of the bacon almost made her moan in delight. Knowing the chef made his own mayonnaise made the sandwich that much better.

She ordered another sandwich for Dirk. Sometimes he didn't take time out of work to eat properly. Marley had noticed the bareness of his fridge yesterday when she'd gone to get them glasses of iced tea. He could do with something this delicious.

After she finished and paid for her and Dirk's orders, Marley headed for the farm in the bottomlands below Misty Hollow. With his sandwich in hand, she went looking for Dirk. She found him measuring spaces in the land he'd chosen for his little community.

Her foot snapped a twig. His head jerked up, and a smile spread across his face. "Hey. What's that in your hand?"

"A sandwich. Now, take a break, tell me what you're doing, and eat." She handed it to him. "Want to go back to the house so I can pour us some tea?"

"Sure, but where's yours?"

"I already ate."

They walked in companionable silence back to the house. The tall grass whispered at their feet. A blue jay squawked from a nearby tree. The peace of the area reinforced the idea that Marley might stay in Misty Hollow. The company of the handsome farmer strolling beside her wasn't unpleasant either.

What would happen between them if she stayed on, after the danger to her had passed? Would the two of them move forward into something deeper than friendship? Her career had kept her from deep relationships for a long time. Slowing down would afford her the opportunity to share her life with someone.

"I'm thinking twenty houses to begin with." Dirk sat at his kitchen table and opened his lunch. I have a decent well, so running water won't be too difficult. I'll get the city to set up the electricity for each site. How are you at gardening?"

"Gardening?" She overpoured a glass of tea and reached for a rag.

"I thought maybe you could make the area around each tiny house look nice." He grinned. "Want to go with me to town to look at a sample? A builder in Langley has several I want to check out. Nothing too big or elaborate. Maybe two-hundred-and-fifty square feet. No more than three for sure."

"Absolutely. That sounds like fun." Maybe she'd find her own patch of land and put her own tiny house on it once her lease was up.

~

Dirk had taken out a second mortgage on the farm in order to have the funds to build his tiny community, but with the added help he'd receive from his residents, he could expand his farm to other crops in addition to rice, then open his studio…God willing, and he'd be able to pay back the mortgage with enough to live well on.

A man could dream big, couldn't he? He pulled

onto the builder's land. Three tiny houses with postage stamp-size porches lined up like little soldiers. He fell in love with all three. Who said all his houses had to look the same?

Marley followed him into the first one. A ladder led to a sleeping loft. A barn door closed off what would be the bathroom. The building was empty of anything else, standing ready for a person to add their personal touch.

He didn't plan on making them fancy. A wet room for the bathroom with a composting toilet. A small kitchenette with a dorm-size fridge, sink, a two-burner stovetop, shelves for storage. Some cubbies for clothes and such. A sofa that would also serve as a bed. Just the necessities. He wanted the people who lived there to want to put their own personal stamp on the homes.

He did some mental calculating in his head. Yes, it was doable. Just barely, with a bit left over to keep the farm going until he had the needed help. "What do you think?" He took Marley's hand.

"I can totally picture your vision. It'll be perfect. How long do you think it will take?"

"Four weeks for delivery of the houses. The man said he has ten ready if they don't have to look the same. While he's building the others, I can work on the first ten. Start bringing people to live in them." He glanced down at her, grateful for someone to share his dream with. "I can get one house livable each week."

"How?" Her eyes widened. "That's a lot of work, in addition to running the farm."

"I'll work late." He could do this. After everything was done, then he'd take a few days off and rest. Maybe go down to Louisiana or Florida and spend some time on the beach.

"Do you like going to the beach, Marley?"

"Love it. If I lived close, I'd be one of those leathery old ladies who spends every day there."

Wonderful. If he was lucky, he'd take her along.

Their next stop was the camper-parts store where he placed his order for the inside plumbing equipment and appliances. When they'd finished, he was a whole lot poorer but a lot happier. "Let's get an ice cream to celebrate a very successful day."

"That sounds wonderful. It's been a long time since I've had ice cream for supper."

"Is it that time already?" He glanced at his watch. "Would you rather have supper?"

"After the mention of ice cream?" She tried to look shocked but failed. "What kind of girl do you take me for?" Her smile faded at something over his shoulder.

He turned. A woman in ragged clothing stared from behind a display of floor rugs. "Do you know her?"

"No, but she seems very interested in us." She slipped her arm in his. "Let's get out of here. Anyone who stares too long makes me nervous. Especially since I don't know what this Annie person looks like."

He took a long look at the woman before letting Marley pull him away. If he saw her again, he'd alert the sheriff. There'd been no fan letters for a few weeks which gave him hope the fan had moved on, leaving Marley safe. This overly curious woman brought back the feeling that the crazed stalker could still be out there…watching. Some of the day's brightness faded.

He drove them to a nearby ice-cream shop in Langley where they both ordered chocolate sundaes.

"Thank you for helping me today."

"I really didn't do much but tag along." She took a big spoonful of the ice cream. "I thought the tiny houses were adorable. You know, I wouldn't mind living in one. Maybe a little bigger though. I'd like something to use for an office with stairs rather than a ladder."

"Really?" He grinned. "Thinking of buying one?"

She nodded. "Yes. I have a few months to decide whether this is where I want to stay or not. A lot of it will depend on my writing, and whether I can do freelance work for the station."

Hope leaped in his heart. He couldn't think of anything better than having her stay in Misty Hollow. Out of all of the folks around town, she was the only one he'd let into his inner circle. Maybe instead of a handshake or a punch, he should give the sheriff a hug for asking him to watch over Marley. Dirk couldn't think of a time he was gladder about being former military PD than at that moment.

Of course, he had no idea he'd use his skills to be a bodyguard of sorts for a beautiful woman in trouble.

Chapter Seven

Annie held her pencil so tight she snapped it in half. What did one write to someone who wasn't following orders? Marley should be making friends with her, not cozying up to a flannel-wearing hillbilly,

Every single day Annie made sure to be at the diner for lunch. Marley *always* ate lunch at the diner. She made it a point to stop and talk to her, pulling her away from the book she shouldn't be writing. If she wrote the book, Annie would have no choice but to do the same thing to Marley that she had the other author.

Rage boiled so hot and furious spots swam in front of her eyes. With sweaty hands, she tossed the broken pencil into the garbage. She wanted Marley as her friend, not lying in a grave.

She swept the papers off the table and watched as they fluttered to the worn carpet like bleached-out leaves. Ugh. Then she folded her arms and rested her head on them. She would simply have to try harder to make friends with Marley. But first...another letter. A warning that she should keep her eyes open for friendship opportunities.

She retrieved the scattered papers and gripped a fresh pencil. *Dear Marley…*

~

Marley almost missed the most recent note. Rather than tape it to the front door, it had been held in place by a rock on the porch railing in the camera's blind spot. Her hand trembled as she removed the rock.

Dear Marley,

I am very glad you're making friends around town, but I think you're making the wrong ones. Why haven't you made friends with me yet? Do you not see me?

I'm always watching. Always nearby. Open your eyes, friend.

Yes, it's a worthwhile thing your friend is trying to do for the community, but your helping him is keeping you from your goal. Me. You don't want anything to happen to the handsome fella, do you?

Also, I shouldn't have to tell you that writing a book of the type you seem set on writing can't possibly be good for you. I'll be in touch. In fact, you might find me to be a bit annoying until you realize how much you need me as your friend.

Annie

Marley swallowed past the boulder in her throat and sagged onto the porch steps. Not only was her life in danger, but Dirk's as well now. She peered in the direction of his farm as if she could see through all the buildings and trees to make sure he was okay.

What should she do? She'd promised him that she

would help him with his tiny-house community. If she showed him the letter, told him she couldn't help, he wouldn't be swayed. She hadn't known him long, but she knew a stubborn streak ran through him. The threat clasped in her hand would only spur him further.

She jumped up and darted down the sidewalk. Sheriff Westbrook would know what to do.

He listened without speaking while she told him about the letter, then held out his hand. "I'd like to read it for myself."

"Okay, but it doesn't tell us anything more than what's written there. Sorry about my fingerprints all over it. I didn't think." She plopped into the chair across from him. "Can you—"

"Shh. Just for a moment, Miss Brooks."

She frowned and clamped her lips, leaning forward when he set the paper down. "Can you have someone watch over Dirk? Should I stop helping him? Maybe I should leave town."

"Miss Brooks." He held up a hand and gave her a patient smile. "Dirk Mason is more than capable of taking care of himself. No, you don't have to stop helping him; nor do you need to leave town." He folded his hands on top of his desk. "Most of the time, stalker fans are nothing more than a nuisance."

"But sometimes they kill." She brought the theme of her novel to his attention.

"Unfortunately, yes. That's why we aren't letting down our guard, but not overreacting either. I will make sure an officer drives by his farm periodically. Same as we have one driving past where you reside. Other than that, until we have an ID on this person, there isn't much more we can do."

"But you're former FBI." She crossed her arms. "You know more than most."

"Maybe." He laughed. "Trust me, Miss Brooks. I will let you know when you really need to start worrying. Although I wouldn't bring this up to Dirk, I would like to know if he ever receives a threat like this."

"So, you're asking me to look out for him like he is for me?"

"In a way, yes. Word around town is the two of you are together every day anyway." He shrugged. "Small-town life. Take my word, ma'am. I will be the first to let you know when things have progressed to a dangerous level. Let's pray it never progresses that far."

"Okay." She took a deep breath.

"Any idea who this Annie is?"

"No. Other than Dirk, I don't know much about anyone. I wouldn't know who is new and who isn't."

"Anyone trying to make friends with you? Someone who seems overly zealous?"

"Not really. I'm used to people coming up to me. Hard not to when you're a celebrity of sorts." It didn't matter where she went, someone spoke to her.

"Stay vigilant. It'll be fine." He stood and escorted her to the door. "Tell Dirk I'll be out sometime to see his progress on the houses."

She promised to pass the word on and headed to the diner. The closer she got, the louder her stomach rumbled. Marley had never been one to skip a meal despite her petite size. She rarely waited until nine to eat breakfast.

Her steps quickened when she spotted Dirk's truck in the diner parking lot. Hopefully, he wasn't finished, and they could eat together.

When she entered, he smiled and waved. Good. Nothing on his table but a glass of water.

She put on a winsome smile. "I didn't expect you this morning."

"Had to mail some things, so I thought I'd grab a bite to eat. Join me?"

"Glad to." She sat.

The server came almost immediately, and Marley ordered biscuits and chocolate gravy.

"Uh-oh." Dirk tilted his head. "Rough morning?"

"I received another letter."

"Can I see it?"

She shook her head. "I turned it over to the sheriff." Marley locked gazes with him. "This one threatened *you*."

~

"Me?" He stiffened. "What does the person have against me?"

"She seems to think I'm spending too much time with you when I should be making friends with her."

"If she doesn't come forward, how do you know who she is?" He shook his head. "This gets crazier all the time. What did the sheriff say?"

"He doesn't think it's time to worry too much yet. Wants me to watch your back while you watch mine."

He grinned. "I've heard of worse things to do."

She giggled, sending his heart racing. "Me, too. Oh, and this Annie person told me not to write my book."

"Are you going to continue?"

"Absolutely. If she is the same person that killed that author, my writing this book might pull her out into the open, and they can arrest her on both counts."

"It sounds to me as if you're using yourself and this book as bait." His smile faded.

"I guess I am. I have less than six months before I have to decide what I'm doing with the rest of my life. I don't want to spend all that time in fear of a knife in my back." She sat against the back of the booth seat as the server placed their orders in front of them.

"Okay, I'm here to help in any way I can. I have an extra room if it comes to the point where you don't feel safe in town."

She laughed, pouring the gravy over her biscuits. "The house of an ex-mob boss is probably the safest place in the state."

He laughed with her. "I think you're right."

After breakfast, they went their separate ways with her promising to come by after lunch to show him her ideas for a simple flower garden by each house. "I also think you should have a community vegetable garden for the people to work in. It would give them a sense of purpose. Pride in something well done."

"You're a genius." He picked up the vinyl for the floors of the houses, then placed an order for vegetable seeds. By planting time next year, he'd have all the help he'd need on the farm and wouldn't be spending a lot out of pocket. At least, he hoped so. He wanted to pay off the second mortgage as quickly as possible and open his studio.

Back at the farm, he carried the floor vinyl into what had once been a barn for farm animals. He studied the area with new eyes. The wood building with a metal roof would make a great self-defense studio once he did some alterations. He'd start here once the houses were ready for occupancy.

Bear padded into the barn and leaned against Dirk's leg. "Hello, boy. Been holding down the fort for me?"

He received a tail wag as a response. Tires crunched outside, drawing him out of the building.

The electrician and plumber had arrived to check out what they'd need to do before the houses were built. Dirk led them to the section of land and walked them through where the houses would be placed. "A setup like you'd find in a campground is what I'm looking for."

"A box and water. Got it." The men moved away to start work, leaving Dirk to finish unloading his truck.

He stared into the truck bed. One of the barrels of glue for the vinyl was no longer there. He marched back to the barn even though he didn't remember unloading the barrel. Not finding it there, he returned to the truck. "What in the heck, boy?" Dirk glanced at Bear who stared into the trees, hackles raised. "Is somebody out there?" He put a hand on the dog's head. Somebody must have thought it funny to steal the glue.

He might still have enough to finish the job without purchasing more, but he'd wanted to be sure he didn't run out in the middle of the work. "Bear, stay." No one would come close with the dog sitting guard. Dirk hefted two barrels out of the bed and returned to the barn.

The next order of business would be padlocks on the doors.

Back at the truck, Bear still stared into the trees. Dirk picked up a crowbar he'd tossed in the back a few days ago. "Come on, boy. Let's run off our visitor."

Keeping the dog close, Dirk entered the darkness of the thick stand of trees. A twig snapped up ahead. "Stop, or I will sic my dog on you."

A thud sounded ahead of them. Dirk increased his pace, keeping a lookout for potential places from where the thief could lie in wait and ambush him. Instead, he found the stolen barrel of glue. The ground was too hard for footprints, but the area looked disturbed as if a foot ready to run had kicked up the forest debris.

"It appears Marley's fan paid us a visit, Bear."

Chapter Eight

After three days of no contact, Marley *almost* thought the harassment had come to an end. Was it possible the woman had given up? Then, she stepped onto her porch and found a box of puppies just old enough to be weaned. Six puppies to be exact.

A sheet of notebook paper lined the bottom of the box. From what Marley could see, it was another letter, this one soiled by the puppies.

"What am I supposed to do with all of you?" She hefted the box into her arms and received a thorough face washing. Laughing, she carried the box inside and set it on the floor in the downstairs bathroom. "No, I'm not letting you have the freedom to destroy this place." She blocked the doorway rather than close the door, and couldn't help staring at the wriggling surprise. "You all look like mutts to me. Let's see what my 'friend' has to say." Using the tips of two fingers, she lifted the soggy paper from the box.

Dear Marley,
This is what friends do. They give each other gifts. Acknowledge they exist. Correspond, communicate, whatever needs to be done to feel accepted and appreciated.

You're a tough nut to crack, Little Missy, but you remind me so much of the daughter I once had that I am willing to work very hard to reach my goal. We will be best friends one day. Wait and see.

I'm aware that you won't keep the puppies, but I found them dumped on the side of the road and knew that someone with a heart as warm as yours would find homes for them.

Oh, before I forget, let Mr. Mason know that I like his choice of vinyl flooring. Looks like wood but more durable. Very nice.
Your friend,
Annie

Marley didn't know what was more frightening, the threatening letters, or this one where Annie assumed they were besties. Maybe she should find a way to communicate with the woman. Write her letters and leave them on the porch? Put up another camera so there weren't any blind spots and find out who the woman really was.

She picked up a puppy, nuzzled it under her chin, and sent Dirk a text that she wouldn't be at the diner as she had six puppies to care for. He responded immediately.

I'm intrigued.
On my way over with doughnuts.

Coffee?

Coffee she could definitely do. She placed the puppy on the floor where it immediately zoomed around the room, black nose to the floor. Maybe Marley would keep the little girl. Surely, her landlord wouldn't mind. She'd send them an email as soon as she could.

The doorbell rang sending six fur balls into furious barking. Shaking her head and grinning, Marley peered through the peephole, then let Dirk in.

"You have puppies?" He grinned at the one bounding at his feet.

"Good morning to you, too." She took the box of doughnuts from his hands so he could pick up the puppy. "Yes, I have six. A present from Annie. The letter is on top of the garbage."

He stood over the trash can, read the letter, then faced Marley. "She's weird."

"Very." She handed him a cup of coffee. "Let me put this little one with the others then you can help me decide what to do with them." She took the puppy and placed it in the bathroom.

"You could put up a sign at Lucy's. They don't look like big dogs, and they're kind of fluffy. Women like frou-frou dogs, don't they? I think they might be long-haired dachshunds."

"Why would someone dump a litter of dachshunds?"

He shrugged. "Maybe Annie stole them."

Her mouth fell open. "You're right. They could belong to someone else. I'll call the sheriff." Maybe the owner would let Marley purchase one of the pups.

Doris, the sheriff's receptionist, confirmed that

someone had reported a litter stolen that morning. "I'll send someone over to get them."

"Could you also let the owner know I'm interested in purchasing one?"

"Will do." Doris hung up.

Marley sighed. "An officer will be by to pick them up."

He gave her a one-armed hug. "If you want a puppy, get one. Someone always has a litter around here."

"I want that one." She pointed to a dapple with one blue eye. "I'm being silly. This isn't even my house, and the next six months are up in the air as to what I'll do."

The doorbell rang. Dirk set his cup on the counter. "Stay."

Marley leaned against the counter and sipped her coffee. "The officer?"

"No." He carried in a vase of yellow roses. "I'd like to say these are from me, but the card says Annie."

Her eyes widened. "She wasn't kidding about the gifts coming. What am I going to do? Do you think maybe I should start communicating with her somehow?"

"That's what she wants. It might keep her from escalating."

"As long as I don't meet her in person, I should be safe enough." She took a pad of paper from a kitchen drawer and carried both it and her coffee to the table. "Now, to figure out how to keep her at arm's length once we are friends." She made quote marks with her fingers over the word, *friends*. "Because I don't want to meet her face-to-face without backup."

~

By the time a police officer arrived at Marley's to pick up the pups, she'd managed to write a short letter to Annie. Since the paper wasn't the same as what the other woman used, she hoped Annie would recognize the letter for what it was.

"I'll order another camera to be installed this week."

Marley nodded. "And I'll contact the owner and take the cost out of my rent. A few days shouldn't make a lot of difference." Dirk hoped it wouldn't. When the doorbell rang again, it was one of the deputies.

As the deputy put the box in his car, she taped the letter to the porch post and said, "Want to meet for lunch later?"

"No, sorry but I won't be back into town today. I scheduled a meeting with the electrician. He's setting up my boxes. I just happened to be here to pick up some supplies when I received your text."

She smiled. "That's good news. I'll bring lunch to you. The special?"

"Sure." No matter what the day's special was, it would be good.

He stopped at his truck. The back left tire was flat. A screwdriver stuck out from the rubber. "Looks like my gifts are different than yours."

Marley paled. "She'll hurt you."

"I won't make it easy." He pulled his phone from his pocket to order a new tire and to let the electrician know he'd be late. The flat tire concerned him some but not a lot. Unless the threats escalated, he'd go with the flow until this Annie was caught.

He reached over and gave Marley's hand a

squeeze. "It'll be fine. I'm going to be so busy over the next few months that we won't be together as much. She'll settle down." He ordered a tire which would be delivered within thirty minutes, made a call to the electrician, then notified the sheriff of the vandalism. When he'd finished, he stared at the house.

"The driveway is not in a blind spot. Where can we watch the footage?"

"The panic room." She flashed a grin. "They have two." She led the way upstairs and through the master room closet.

Soon, they watched as a woman in baggy clothes, big sunglasses, and a floppy hat stabbed the screwdriver into Dirk's tire. "Can't tell anything other than the fact it's a woman and she did, in fact, flatten my tire."

"We already suspected Annie was a woman." She peered closer at the screen. "Something about her seems familiar, but I can't figure out what."

"It'll come to you." A horn outside alerted them that his tire was here.

They moved back to his truck. Dirk changed the tire and sped to the farm. As he drove, his mind focused on the woman. *Annie.* What could he tell from the footage? A Caucasian woman around five foot four inches tall. He couldn't tell her age or if she were thin or curvy under all the clothes she wore.

Why start sending Marley friendly gifts and leave him a threatening one? He'd shrugged off the theft of the glue earlier, but now he realized she was sending him a warning, and he needed to take heed of it. What would she do if he didn't?

Dirk had been right about his schedule being busy, but he had second thoughts about not seeing Marley as much. Safety in numbers. If Marley was with him, Annie couldn't get to her without going through him. That wouldn't be easy.

The electrician had two boxes installed by the time Dirk joined him. He peered at the two rows of ten cement slabs. Off to his right, the building kits had started to arrive. His dream was quickly taking shape. Dirk needed to do two things: keep Marley safe from Annie and keep Annie away from destroying his tiny houses.

He wouldn't put it past the woman. At some point, she'd start striking at what was important to him. Marley topped that list, but right now, Marley was also at the top of Annie's list. As long as she stayed in the Victorian, she was safe. That left the houses and his farm.

A perimeter of lights and cameras would help. So would another couple of dogs. He'd make sure they were trained guard dogs. It wouldn't be hard for him to adopt a couple of retired military K-9s. He knew of a former comrade that could help there.

"Can you handle a couple of friends, Bear? Extra help watching over this place?"

Bear's big eyes gazed up at him.

"Good boy."

~

Annie cleaned the last room of the day. The bikers had arrived that morning. When they left for mealtimes, she barely had enough time to get through all the rooms. She'd been too busy all day to head to the diner and catch a glimpse of Marley.

After flattening the farmer's tire, she'd hurried back to the hotel to start her busy day. All she wanted to do now was fall into bed, but she needed to leave another gift. Annie glanced at the leather journal on her nightstand. That was it—something lovely for Marley to write her thoughts and feelings in.

Anything to keep her distracted from writing that book!

She grabbed the journal, locked her room, and set off at a quick pace toward Marley's house.

A yellow sheet of paper fluttered from the porch post.

Expecting an ambush, Annie froze. When one didn't come, she placed the journal on the top step, taking care not to reveal her face. She stretched out one arm to take the sheet of paper from the door, then dashed down the steps and fled under a streetlight.

Dear Annie,

Thank you for thinking of me in such a way, but please promise me you won't steal again in order to gain my friendship. Let's take this slow, getting to know each other. Let our friendship build and bubble with the comfort of homemade soup.
I'll leave my letters to you on the front door.
Here's to a lifelong friendship.

Marley

Annie shot a glance at Marley's front door. This was what she'd been wanting. For Marley to know she existed, that Annie was important to her...valued by someone. She hugged the letter to her chest and practically skipped back to the hotel. Almost immediately, she fell asleep holding tight to the letter and dreaming of a future where she and Marley saw each other on a regular basis. Like friends.

Chapter Nine

The roar of the motorcycles as they left the Misty Motel filled the air. Then, blessed silence. Annie released her breath in a long hiss. The rally ran that day and the next, then all those who created work for her would be gone. She'd have a lot more time to woo Marley into a cemented friendship and make her see that hanging with a rice farmer was a waste of her time. The man would never be good enough for Marley.

Annie grabbed her cleaning supplies from the designated closet. If she hurried with the rooms, she might make it to some of the rally. She'd heard there would be live bands, food, races, and a motorcycle show. She'd never been to such a thing. Plus, she wanted to go by Marley's and see whether she'd written a letter on the new stationery Annie had left for her.
And, she grinned at the thought of the gift she'd left for the farmer.

~

When Marley had asked if the news station would consider her doing freelance work in the future, she hadn't expected to receive an immediate email asking her to cover the local biker rally. Since she was staying in Misty Hollow and this was the town's first rally with over seventy-five bikers converging on the town, she'd been asked to cover the event.

A biker rally? She didn't know the first thing about motorcycles except she'd always wanted to learn how to drive one.

She was meeting Dirk at the rally at noon for lunch and to see what the event was all about, so getting enough information to write an article wouldn't be difficult. She'd find the person in charge, interview them as well as a few others, snap a couple of pictures with her phone, and she could whip up the article in less than an hour. Why not?

Marley sent them a confirmation email letting them know the articles would be in their inbox by Monday morning. A quick glance outside let her know she'd received no new gifts, and her letter to Annie still hung on the door.

A text from Dirk stopped her on the porch. Someone blew up an outhouse? She frowned, her eyes darting up and down the street. Would Annie really do something like that? Maybe Marley needed to inform her that Dirk was off limits to gifts and threats of any kind.

She yanked the letter from the door and carried it to the kitchen where she added:

P.S. I'm upset about the prank with Dirk's porta-potty. If our friendship is to grow, you must leave him alone. He is trying to do a good thing out there.

No more threats, no more nasty gifts, no more

visits. He is my friend, same as you want to be, and I am very protective of my friends.

I won't say this again.

Annie might take offense at Marley's "warning," but it had to be said. If she didn't stop the threats to Dirk, then Marley would stop the charade. They could find another way to catch the crazy woman.

Marley taped the letter back on the door and drove to Dirk's farm. She could smell the problem as soon as she exited her car. She pulled a roll-on perfume from her purse and spread it across her upper lip before going in search of Dirk. She found him exactly where she thought he'd be—at the scene of the crime.

Dirk held the collar of his tee shirt over his nose. Excrement splattered across the nearest cement slabs. Gagging, he stepped away from the scene and placed a call to the sheriff, only then noticing Marley. "Let's get away from this stench." He patted his leg for Bear to follow and led her to the front of the house.

She stood patiently to the side as he told the sheriff the latest. He hung up and smiled. "I can't believe you came out here after what happened."

She laughed. "I've never seen anything like this. Too bad it isn't newsworthy."

"Folks around here will think it is. Write something up and send it to the *Misty Hollow Gazette*."

"I've already been asked to do something on the rally." She leaned against her car. This might be the opportunity she'd been looking for. Freelance for local and state news. Build a platform to help in selling her novel. "Okay, I'll do it." She'd visit the news office with the article in hand and hopefully get herself a job.

Goodbye, big city. Marley was staying in Misty Hollow.

She marched back to the scene and snapped pictures with her phone and told Dirk of what she'd added to Annie's letter. "I won't have her destroy your hard work."

"I appreciate that, but we do want to catch her. The authorities will only be able to do that if she comes out into the open."

"You're doing something for the community. No crazy person should destroy this." She crossed her arms. "I'm still playing the game, Dirk. I simply said I wouldn't if she continued. What if the bomb she used on the outhouse had gone off when someone was nearby or inside? She could've hurt someone."

"It went off at night. She doesn't want to hurt anyone."

"Except you."

His brow furrowed. "She hasn't made a direct attack on me. No, she doesn't plan on doing more than being a nuisance."

"Well, I've already left the note."

A roar filled the air.

~

A long string of motorcycles riding side by side came down the road, stretching further than Dirk could see. The first in line pulled into the driveway and came to a stop in front of him.

"Howdy." Dave, the local motorcycle-club leader, wrinkled his nose. "Septic problems, Dirk? I could smell it a mile away. It's ruining the ambiance of a leisurely scenic drive."

"Sorry." He explained what had happened. "You

heading up the mountain? The odor should dissipate by the time you reach the top." He clapped the other man on the shoulder. "At least you can hope so."

Dave chuckled. "We can hope. Need me to do anything? We helped bring down a crime boss. I'm sure we could help with this."

"No, we're fine. Thanks. I'll hire someone to clean this up, and we'll see you at the rally around noon." He jerked his head toward Marley. "She's writing an article on the town's first rally, so she'll most likely want to speak with you at some point."

"Hunt me up at the food court at noon." He walked the bike back a few feet, then joined the long line waiting for him.

Marley stood next to Dirk and snapped a picture. "All those engines together are exciting. Makes my heartbeat faster."

"Are you a thrill seeker?" He grinned and arched a brow.

"No, but I could be." Her gaze followed an arriving van. "I'm already living in a thriller novel."

"It's my buddy, Luke, from our military days." He strode over to greet his friend.

"Dude. The smell."

"I know. Sorry about that. It shouldn't happen again if you brought my dogs."

"I did. Meet Duke and Luke." He laughed. "Yeah, I share a name with a dog." He opened the van's side door and two Belgian Malinois leaped out. They took up a stance and stared down Bear.

"Is this going to be a problem?" Dirk put a hand on his dog's head.

"Not by the time I leave. These boys are well

trained. Once they're familiar with the people and animals that belong here, they'll only bother those that don't." He handed Dirk a list. "Command words. No one will be able to exit their car without the right word."

Dirk turned to meet Marley's stern gaze. "What?"

"I don't like that you're having to live like this because I came to town."

"It's just dogs, sweetheart. I like dogs." He went over the word and hand commands with Luke, then watched his friend drive away. "Besides, they're only temporary."

They definitely couldn't be here when the residents moved in. What use would the dogs be if everyone in town learned of the word command to bypass the dogs? In a town like Misty Hollow, word always got around.

Before he could lead the dogs to the building site, a trained cleaning crew arrived to tackle the mess. "I guess we're free to go to the rally. No one will be working today, even after that crew finishes. I'll put these two on the porch." He'd find out soon enough whether they'd listen to him. If they were gone by the time he returned, they hadn't.

He planned on taking Bear with him to the rally. The big dog loved crowds. "Is it okay if he goes with us?"

"Why wouldn't it be?" She cast a wary glance at Bear.

"You don't seem to be a big fan."

"I haven't been around dogs much, especially big dogs. He seems all right." Despite her words, she gave Bear a wide berth on the way to the passenger side of Dirk's truck. "I did like the dachshunds."

True. She'd get used to Bear. She climbed in before he could help her. Bear leaped in and sat between them, staring out the front window with his tongue lagging.

Dirk told Marley about meeting with Dave at noon. "Since we're arriving earlier than expected, we can stroll around a little. Soak up the ambiance."

"That will help with the article. Sounds good." She slid from the truck. Bear followed.

Whether Marley was fond of the dog or not, Bear seemed to have taken to her. Seeing that relieved some of the tension Dirk held with regard to Marley's safety. Especially in a crowd like they'd have today. No one would get close to her with Bear around. "Buy him a hot dog, and he'll love you forever."

"I'll do that." Marley patted the dog's head. "A great big one."

Folks called out greetings as they made their way slowly to the food court. Dirk veered off the path to the motorcycle show, marveling at a Harley.

"Dirk?"

He dragged his attention to Marley.

"Look at Bear."

The dog's hackles were raised, his legs stiff. He didn't care for someone near to them.

Dirk turned in a slow circle, trying to find someone in the crowd that seemed too interested in them. "Find," he whispered. "Slow."

Bear slipped into the crowd, his eyes on something Dirk couldn't see.

Dirk took Marley's hand and pulled her close. "Try to act natural. Bear can sneak up on whoever it is while they watch us." He put an arm around her shoulders, not only to keep her close, but to keep Annie's attention—if it was her watching— them and not the dog.

Marley didn't protest. Instead, her hand clutched his shirt. "I shouldn't have come. I shouldn't have said I'd do the article. It's foolish to be in such a big crowd."

"No one can get to you. Not with me and Bear here." He agreed they were taking a huge risk by being at the rally. It wouldn't be difficult for someone to sneak through and stick a knife in his back. All they'd have to do was lure his dog away. Not hard if food was the lure, and there was plenty of food at the rally.

Chapter Ten

Stupid dog! Annie hid in one of the porta-potties until the dog stopped sniffing around. The mutt was most likely confused by the myriad of odors coming from the disgusting plastic box. The dog had come very close to exposing Annie. She'd thought with a crowd as large as this one, she could hide undetected. But she'd gotten too close. Let off some kind of vibe the dog didn't like.

She stepped from the stinking, too hot box. "Marley?" She grinned, a little embarrassed that she'd been caught leaving the restroom. "I didn't expect to see you in this crowd."

"Hello, Jane. Dirk, this is my friend, Jane. Jane, Dirk." Marley gave her a smile so sweet that Annie had to choke back a sob. She'd called her a friend.

"Nice to meet you." The man flashed a handsome grin. "You didn't happen to see a big dog go past, did you?"

"I was…uh." She waved a hand toward the porta-potty.

"Right. Sorry. Maybe we'll run into you again."

He tugged Marley after him, giving a shrill whistle that made heads turn.

Stepping out in front of them was the best thing to happen despite the surroundings. Now, the farmer knew her face, her name, and that Marley called her *friend*. He wouldn't be suspicious if he caught her around.

They all lived in a small town where folks met regularly as they went about their lives. Annie could now openly be where Marley was. No more fading into the background. She could openly be friends with Marley.

~

Thankfully, Bear returned shortly after their meeting Jane. Marley had a job to do and didn't have time to be chasing after a dog that might be chasing after…someone. Since neither she nor Dirk had seen anyone suspicious, the dog could've been trailing a child with an ice cream cone.

"Good boy." Dirk ruffled the dog's fur. "We need to hurry to meet Dave."

Marley nodded and headed for the food court. Since she didn't know what the man looked like, she waited for Dirk to point him out.

"Dave!" Dirk waved.

A massive, bald man marched toward them. "I was about to head out."

"Sorry. Dave, this is Marley. She's the one writing the article."

"I got a few minutes." He gave her a nod and led them to a wood picnic table.

"Thank you." Marley sat across from him and pulled her laptop from her bag.

Dirk offered to get the three of them nachos and

left them alone.

"I understand this is your first rally in Misty Hollow." She smiled. "Tell me about it. Why here? And what are your hopes?"

He crossed his muscled arms on the tabletop. "Me and the boys, the ones who live in Misty Hollow, wanted to give back to those who have done the same before. Some folks look at motorcycle clubs as thugs." He grinned. "We can be, but we ain't. This rally is to show them that. Despite the fact we've helped the sheriff on multiple occasions bring down a bad guy, folks are still a little wary around us."

She could understand that. Seeing all the tough-looking, leather-wearing men and women was intimidating.

"We'll give whoever blew up Dirk's outhouse a thorough pounding when we find them."

Her eyes widened. "You plan on looking for them?"

He gave a long, slow nod, his eyes narrowing. "We look after our own in this town."

"Maybe someday I'll be in that circle." She typed on the keyboard.

"You're a friend of Dirk's. That's all we need."

"Then keep an eye out for my crazy-stalker fan." She closed her laptop.

"You have a stalker?" His features hardened.

Marley hadn't meant to say anything out loud. She'd meant her words to be flippant. After giving him the condensed version, she glanced up to see Dirk with a tray and three plates of nachos.

"We'll keep an eye on you. Thanks, man, but I've already eaten. No time for a second lunch." He pushed to his feet. "I look forward to the article, ma'am."

Marley watched him walk away. Jane stepped in line at a corn-dog stand. "Why not let her have the extra nachos?"

Dirk followed her gaze. "I suppose we could. Better than going to waste." He headed for the woman, then returned with Jane right behind him.

Tears filled Jane's eyes as she sat down. "Thank you."

Was the woman so lonely that a simple request to join someone for lunch would make her cry? "Glad to have you."

Jane kept up a lively conversation about the Misty Motel and some of the people who had stayed there. "I can't give you names because that's breaching a confidence, but working at the motel is definitely entertaining. You should write an article about it, Marley. It would make a good human-interest piece."

Maybe. "I'll think about it. See if it interests the *Gazette*'s editor." The man hadn't responded to her yet about being a freelance reporter. She wasn't one for fluff pieces, but they'd fill the pages when something bigger wasn't happening. Marley made a mental note to pay the man a visit in person on Monday.

After eating, Marley threw the cardboard plates away. "I have a job to do. See you around, Jane."

The woman clapped her hands. "I'll be looking forward to it. It isn't every day that someone like me has a famous celebrity as a friend."

She wasn't the first person to fawn over Marley, but having someone look at her as if she was different than them made her uncomfortable. She gave Jane a thin smile and headed toward the first live band.

~

"What's wrong?" Dirk caught up with her as she sat in a folding chair.

"I don't like fawning." She shifted in her seat. "The woman wants to be my friend so badly, but if she treats me as if I'm better than she, I won't want to be around her. So, when people start acting that way, I walk away. It's a defense move, I guess."

He nodded and bumped her with his shoulder. "I promise to treat you like a fellow farmer."

She giggled. "Thanks."

"—Who happens to be a famous news reporter."

"Stop." Her laughter grew, drawing attention to them.

Just then Jane strolled past them searching for a seat. Not finding one next to them, she turned and headed back.

Good. Having Jane sit next to Marley after Marley had walked away would be uncomfortable. He glanced over his shoulder and smiled. Jane sat three rows back, her gaze glued to the stage as the band took their places.

Bear kept shooting growls behind them so often that the hair on Dirk's neck stood on end. Marley's stalker, or whoever had bothered the dog earlier, also sat under the tent to watch the band. Dirk fought the urge to stand up and study every face until the stalker's jumped out at him.

"What's wrong?" Marley shot him a quick glance.

"Just a feeling. Bear has it, too."

She peered behind them. "Nobody looks suspicious to me. I doubt anyone is going to do either of us harm with this many people around."

True, but he didn't like it. He tried to enjoy the

music. Dirk had heard worse heavy metal, but the feeling that danger sat very close to them wouldn't go away. When Marley said she'd had enough twenty minutes later, he couldn't be more relieved.

"Want to go look at the cool bikes?" He put a hand on the small of her back, liking the way it fit. How natural it seemed.

"Sure. I'd also like to get some quotes from other bikers and attendees. That way I can gauge how well Dave's first rally went."

"Here's one indication." He drew her attention to where several men in leather started throwing punches and shouts. "Looks like a rival gang showed up uninvited."

"How can you possibly know that?" She started taking pictures with her phone.

"Because I heard one guy tell another guy that he hadn't been invited and had a lot of nerve showing up."

"You have good hearing." She headed toward them.

"No way. You aren't getting involved." He grabbed her arm.

"This would be great for my article." She yanked free.

"Your stalker can get to you easily in a brawl. It'll look like an accident."

She shook her head and kept walking. "She isn't ready to harm me."

Of all the stubborn women, she had to be at the top of the list. Dirk hurried to catch up, Bear on his heels, and followed Marley into the melee of cursing and flying fists.

A fist connected with the side of his head, bringing

stars to his eyes. He reached for Marley, intending to pull her free of the mob. As his fingers brushed her arm, she fell.

"Get away from her!" He shouldered his way to her side, doing his best to avoid the gauntlet of flying fists and feet. Reaching her, he scooped her into his arms and fought their way free.

"Are you okay?" He set her on her feet then caught her when she started to fall.

"Someone hit me, then someone else stepped on my ankle."

He carried her to the food court and set her on a table. "Let me see." Dirk didn't have a lot of medical training, but he could tell whether her ankle was broken or not. He gently turned her foot this way and that. "Not broken. Definitely bruised." He lightly touched her face where a bruise already showed on her cheekbone. With his thumb, he wiped blood from her bottom lip. "That's going to look pretty in a few days."

"Not my first black eye."

Curiosity rose. He opened his mouth to ask for details, when the sheriff strode their way.

"Heard Marley was injured in the scuffle."

"I'm fine, Sheriff." She hopped off the table. "I'll have a limp for a day or two."

"Did you see who hit you?"

"No, and it doesn't matter. Wrong place at the wrong time."

He turned his attention on Dirk. "I can't believe you let her get in that mess."

"Short of tying her up, I tried to stop her." He frowned. "She's writing an article on the rally." He didn't like being accused of negligence.

"Nobody can make me do anything I don't want." Marley put her hands on her hips. "Rather than harass Dirk, you need to find my stalker."

"We're doing our best. She's good at staying out of sight."

"I think she's in plain sight," Dirk said. "Probably watching us right now. She's close and getting closer."

As if he could find her, the sheriff turned and studied the crowd. "I agree. She's here. There is no way she would have stayed away. Not when she could walk right up to Marley with no one the wiser. Finish your article, Miss Brooks, and head home." Without looking back, he melted into the crowd.

"He's right. I should have stopped you." Dirk put an arm around her waist. "Let me know if I need to carry you."

"I'm fine. I can put my foot up while I write the article."

He drove her home, helped her to the sofa, then went to the kitchen for ice. He dropped some into a baggy, then wrapped a dishtowel around it before placing it gently on her ankle. "I'll get some more ice for your eye."

"No need. I'll switch this one back and forth. Thank you." She smiled up at him.

He lowered his head and kissed her. "You aren't as tough as you think you are."

She smiled against the kiss. "I'm a whole lot smarter than you think I am."

Good. Because the time was coming when she'd have to prove it.

Chapter Eleven

Annie used her card key to enter room number twelve. The man who had struck Marley would have to pay for his crime. He'd marred her beautiful face, even split her lip.

Heavy snoring greeted her when she entered the room. Good. The sleeping pills she'd slipped into his beer while he showered had knocked him out good.

She took her time tying his hands and feet together, then gagged him. By this time, his eyes were fluttering. He wouldn't stay asleep much longer. Perfect. She wanted him awake when he paid for what he'd done. She wanted him to feel pain as Marley had.

The man's eyes popped open. He whimpered under the gag.

"A big man like you squealing like a girl?" She arched a brow and pulled a chair closer to the bed. "I'm having second thoughts now. My dear friend—the one you punched in the face this afternoon—won't like that I'm here to kill you." More squealing. "But, now that you've seen my face, what can I do? I was going to cut off the hand that punched her…" she shrugged. "That would only alert the sheriff that it had something to do with the fight."

She exhaled slowly. "So, I'm going to make it look like retaliation from one of your rivals. You'll still be dead, I'll have my satisfaction, and my friend will be avenged."

He started to buck on the bed, causing the headboard to bang the wall. "If you don't stop trying to attract attention, I will start cutting off pieces." She shoved against the bed and moved it a couple of inches from the wall.

"Let's get started." She retrieved a baseball bat from outside the door, glanced around to make sure no one loitered outside, then locked the door and exacted her revenge on the man.

~

Marley read over the chapter she'd written the day before. Ten chapters in and thirty-thousand words. And then she hit a brick wall. She didn't know what happened next. The author wasn't around to question, and Marley's circumstances were still playing out.

She sipped her coffee and stared at the trees behind the house. The view would never get old. A cardinal flitted in and out of the trees, finally coming to rest on a bird feeder Marley had set up a few days ago. Soon, a blue jay joined the cardinal. She definitely wouldn't get any writing done by watching the birds.

A siren's wail pierced the peace of the morning then faded into the distance. With a sigh, she pushed to her feet and carried her coffee and laptop to the kitchen table. She checked the front porch, surprised and relieved not to find a letter from Annie. No letter meant no reply needed.

She reopened her laptop and stared at the blank page of a new chapter. Her protagonist, a female detective, had also hit a brick wall in her investigation. Marley could make stuff up—it was a fictional retelling—but the words wouldn't come.

A bit of breakfast might help her figure out the next plot point. She locked up the house and headed to the diner. With the next book, she'd definitely have to start writing pure fiction. Annie was taking her time asking for a face-to-face meeting, which, Marley could put in her book, but then what? Back to the brick wall.

The diner was abuzz about something. "What happened?" She followed the hostess to a booth.

"Somebody tied up one of those biker guys and beat him to death with a baseball bat out at the Misty Motel." She shook her head. "That means war. His group will think the other group did it, and they'll want revenge."

"Maybe that won't happen."

"I don't know." She glanced to where Dave and two of his friends entered the diner. The men surveyed the room, then turned and shoved past Jane who was trying to come in. Moments later they roared from the parking lot. Jane frowned their way, then smiled when she caught sight of Marley.

Marley sighed and took her seat, waving the woman toward her booth. "Join me?"

"I'd be delighted. What's up with those men? I've never known them to be rude before."

"One of their men was brutally murdered. My guess is they're looking for the likely culprit."

Jane's eyes widened. "The other biker gang?"

"Who knows? Wait a minute. Didn't you hear

anything at the motel this morning?"

"No, I left early. It's my day off. I get out of there as fast as possible before they rope me into working." She glanced at the front window. "I must have left before the sheriff's department arrived."

Sheriff Westbrook entered the diner. When conversation increased with a barrage of questions, he put his fingers to his lips and gave a shrill whistle. "Folks, we're enacting a six-p.m. curfew for the next few days, but, I suggest you not wander the streets at any time of the day."

"Is it war?" Someone shouted.

"It's shaping up to be." He took another look around the room, then left.

"This is bad." Marley reached for a menu.

"You should be safe enough in that big house of yours."

Her hand froze. "How do you know where I live?"

Jane laughed. "Everyone knows you rented the mob-boss house. You're a celebrity, thus big news."

Marley frowned. "I'll be glad when people are used to me being here and don't care so much about what I do." She chose a ham-and-cheese omelet.

"I'd best be going." Jane slid from the booth. "I only came in to see what all the uproar was about. I was walking by when the bikers sped into the parking lot. Looked suspicious." She flashed a smile. "See you around."

What a strange woman.

~

Dirk wiped his greasy hands on an equally greasy rag and went to greet the bikers pouring onto his land. "Hey, Dave."

"Have you seen any of the gang we fought with yesterday?" The man's eyes flashed.

"No, I haven't left my property today. Too much to do."

"Then you don't know there's a curfew going on. Not that me and the boys will pay much attention to it. Westbrook put it in place to keep the community safe, not us."

"What happened?" Horror filled him as he heard of the dead biker. "You really think one of your rivals killed him?"

"Who else?" He growled. "Let us know if you see any of them hanging around."

"I would've thought they'd have left after the rally."

"So did I." He started his bike and led the others away.

Dirk shook his head. "I'm not liking this at all, Bear." He glanced to where Duke and Luke sat watching the bikers head away from them. They would let him know if someone showed up.

He didn't think they'd come to the farm, but there was a lot of government land surrounding his place. A big area for a few men to hide out in. When he finished working on the tractor, again, he'd take the dogs out to sniff around.

Sounds from behind the house filled him with joy—proof that work continued on the tiny houses. Things were moving along just fine. Once a few houses were ready for occupancy, he'd head to the homeless camp on the other side of the lake and offer an invitation to any who were veterans. Maybe someday, he'd build more houses for any who were homeless and needed a fresh start.

With thoughts of the future swirling through his head, he couldn't help but think about Marley. He really hoped she'd stick around. If the bikers did get into a full-fledged war, she might leave right along with other residents of Misty Hollow.

Dave had always seemed like a level-headed guy. Maybe if Westbrook sat down and spoke with him… Dirk glanced up as the bikers sped by again, this time headed up the mountain. No, Dave wouldn't listen until he'd had time to cool off. If a fight broke out, tempers would flare, and reason would vanish.

The sheriff department would need help. After washing up in the house, he drove into town to offer his services as a temporary deputy.

"I'm much obliged, Dirk." The sheriff waved him into a conference room. "Others have volunteered as well—good men who have helped in the past—and we can definitely use a former military PD. We're meeting in here. I'm sorry to pull you away from Miss Brooks, but this takes priority."

Not to him. Somehow, he'd manage to do both. Dirk nodded at the others in the conference room and sat.

"There should be no one out after six unless they're heading to or from work. No one walking anywhere. Period. Straight to their destination. If someone refuses to comply, they will be fined." The sheriff planted his palms flat on the table. "This could get real ugly, guys. More people might die before this is over. Don't do anything rash. We aren't here to be heroes. We're here to protect the public. Got it?" His gaze went from man to man as heads nodded.

The meeting didn't last long. Dirk stepped outside in time to see Marley, a grocery bag in her hand, limp past. He jogged to catch up with her.

"Hey."

"Hey." She smiled. "Getting some necessities since I'll be locked up in the evenings for a while. Good thing my landlord has an extensive library, otherwise boredom looms."

"Yeah." He walked with her to her house. "Heed the curfew, okay? No matter what."

Her brow furrowed. "I'm not an idiot, Dirk."

"No, just headstrong at times."

Her face darkened. "I appreciate your concern, but if I was stupid enough to violate curfew, that would be *my* business."

"That means no outside, period. I've been deputized and will enforce this, even with you."

She rolled her eyes. "Don't get too big for your britches, *Deputy*." She spun around and headed to her front door, entering without looking back or waving.

He hadn't meant to make her mad, but he was serious. If someone wanted to harm her, they could easily get to her in the backyard. Staying inside was the best thing for her and would allow him to focus on the job he had to do.

At six that night, he reported in with the sheriff; then with Bear beside him, he drove up and down the streets of Misty Hollow. The town had an eerie stillness about it—one that made his skin prickle. He'd thought danger had come with Marley's arrival. That was nothing compared to what loomed on the horizon with the biker's murder.

A shadow darted around the corner of the

drugstore. Dirk cut his lights and cruised past, straining to see in the dark. Whoever it was knew to stay out from under the streetlights.

He parked the truck a few spaces away from a rusty sedan. "Come on, Bear. Find." He checked the ammo in his handgun, grabbed a flashlight from the glove compartment, then followed the dog.

Bear would sniff for a few feet, then stop and sniff the air, his ears twitching, then move a few more feet.

"What's wrong, boy?" Dirk shined a light ahead of them. It wasn't like Bear to be so hesitant.

No footprints on the cement. Of course, there wouldn't be unless someone had mud on their feet, and it hadn't rained in a while. The stillness of the night continued to send ants down his spine. Something was off. Where were the bikers? Holed up somewhere planning their next move, or had they decided a war wasn't worth the effort?

Either way, the quiet and the fleeing dark figure spooked him. No way was he dumb enough to allow himself to be cornered by going after someone alone. He'd call for backup. As he headed back to his truck, he reached for his radio to make the call.

Then the sedan to his right exploded.

Dirk flew off his feet and landed, hard, on the sidewalk.

Twelve

Oh, this was going to be fun! Annie picked herself up off the ground. *She* hadn't planted the bomb in the old car, but wanted to applaud whoever did. Annie cast a glance toward the farmer, then darted away, grabbing the bag she'd dropped due to the explosion.

She'd keep the deputy farmer so busy he wouldn't know whether to save the town or Marley. Then, Annie would swoop in to rescue her, sealing their friendship. Plus, sending Marley into hiding would protect her from the coming Armageddon.

A man holding a Molotov cocktail whirled in her direction. This man wasn't from the local biker group. She dashed between two buildings before she became part of the scene and took the back alleys. Another explosion shattered the silence from the area she'd just left. The rival gang seemed intent on burning Misty Hollow to the ground.

She was more than happy to help.

~

Marley stared at the orange glow in the direction of

the town. Was Dirk in the middle of it? Her heart lurched, thinking of the danger he'd voluntarily put himself in. Here she was idle and incapable of helping, although the gang war would add some exciting fodder for her book.

As she started to close the window blinds, someone in a dark hoodie and ski mask stepped under one of the streetlights. Marley peered closer as the person lit something in their hand. Seconds later, an explosion set the porch railing on fire.

The perpetrator didn't look like a biker. On the small side, like a woman. Annie.

Marley closed the blinds and raced for the door under the stairs. She yanked it open, then closed it behind her, hunching over in order to go through the secret panel and into a fireproof safe room.

Inside, she slid the iron bolt in place and booted up the monitors. The woman had thrown another Molotov cocktail at the house. It had to be Annie, because she didn't appear to be focused on any other house but the Marley's. Marley should've gotten a dog. Maybe she'd have had some warning.

She flinched at another explosion and prayed the house was as safe as depicted in the monitors. Otherwise, she'd entered her coffin rather than a room designed to protect her. Marley reached for the landline, hoping the fires outside hadn't burned the wires, and called the sheriff's department.

"Are you safe?" The operator asked.

"I think so."

"Then stay where you are. Every available officer is busy in town. There's a bit of a war going on, if you hadn't heard."

"I have, but this woman is burning down the house. It isn't my house!" Guilt assaulted her. It was all her fault. The Victorian would be destroyed simply because Marley rented it.

Her book! "Thank you," She said, then hung up and left the room.

Once under the stairs, she sniffed. Some smoke, but it didn't seem that the fire had entered the house yet. She darted from the closet and snatched her laptop off the kitchen table.

Should she head back to the safe room or seek shelter away from the house? Was anywhere in Misty Hollow safe at this time?

She stared at the front door as the porch roof collapsed. Then, she focused on the wall. Why hadn't the fire burned through yet?

Of course. She smiled. A crime boss with lots of money would've thought of everything, even a fireproof house. But for how long? It would most likely withstand the fire long enough for a person to enter one of the two safe rooms or flee.

Marley longed to flee. The flames licking at the windows made her second-guess the safety of the house.

Something pounded the window behind her.

She screamed and whipped around.

Jane, hand plastered to the glass, motioned for her to unlock the back door.

Knees shaking, Marley let her in. "Why are you here? The town is under curfew."

"I was going home from work and saw the house on fire. Since your car is in the driveway, I figured you'd be home. Let's get out of here." She grasped

Marley's arm.

"I think this house is fireproof."

Jane's eyes widened. "Really?"

"Yes. It doesn't seem to be penetrating past the porch. There is no safer place than here." She set her laptop back on the table before going into the pantry. "Since I have help, you can assist me." She handed Jane a fire extinguisher. "We'll take care of this ourselves. If we can't, the fire will hopefully burn itself out."

"Great idea." Jane sprinted outside, leaving Marley to follow.

It took more than the two fire extinguishers, but after emptying them, Marley turned the water hose on the wall. Soon, there was nothing more to show for the fire but a collapsed roof and smoke-stained walls.

"Thanks for your help. Would you like a cup of coffee?"

"Sure." Jane followed her into the house. "I can't stay long, though. I have to work in the morning."

"Just one cup." Marley measured coffee grounds on top of the filter. "I really am thankful for the assistance. Seeing you helped me think more rationally. I should've gone out with the extinguisher as soon as I realized the house wouldn't burn."

"Still easier with two." Jane grinned, sitting at the table. She glanced around the room. "Fancy house."

"Very. Too fancy for me, but the price was good." She leaned against the counter. "I should be out there on the street. I'm a reporter. This—" she waved her arm in the direction of Main Street. "is what we live for. As soon as I drink this coffee, I'm heading to town with a camera."

"What about the curfew?"

"I've a bit of freedom with a reporter badge. The news will always need to be told." Too bad she'd offered Jane coffee. If she hadn't, she'd be down on Main Street by now, alone, instead of making small talk with a woman she could barely tolerate.

~

Sheriff Westbrook approached Dirk who leaned against a light pole. "You okay?"

"Yeah." He bit back a groan. "I didn't fall far. Might've bruised a rib." It felt like a knife in his side if he took a deep breath.

"I'll take your statement tomorrow. Do you need to go home? Because if you don't, I need you. We have buildings on fire and a gang of bikers headed this way. There's going to be a fight with hell as a backdrop."

Not a vision Dirk wanted to see. "I'm good." He straightened and whistled for Bear to jump into the truck.

"Keep your radio on. We'll need open communication. You can stay in your truck and call us if you see something that needs our help."

"I'll call you if I can't handle it on my own." Pain pierced his side as he climbed into the driver's seat.

Firemen sprayed hoses on a building across the street. An orange glow filled the sky over Main Street. Dirk prayed the town would survive. One fire, sometimes two, burned on each street within a mile radius. He drove up and down them trying to find the arsonist. Neighbors helped neighbors keep the fires from spreading by using water hoses. The businesses weren't as lucky and had to wait for the fire department.

His cell phone rang, and he put it on speaker to

leave his hands free. "Hello."

"Oh, good. I saw the fires and wanted to make sure you were okay."

He smiled knowing that Marley cared enough. "I'm good. You?"

"Good. Had a bit of a scare earlier. I'll fill you in later, but it's all good now." He glanced from side to side as he drove.

He slowed at an intersection. To his right, the road ended at a burning building. Standing in front of the building was a woman whose silhouette looked like Marley. *You've got to be kidding!* She turned to reveal her profile.

"You ready to turn in?" He narrowed his eyes.

"Yeah, it's been a heck of a few hours, and I'm beat."

Dirk eased his door open and exited the truck. "I still have a long night in front of me."

"Poor thing."

"Yeah, poor thing. Look to your right."

She turned. "Oh."

He waved when she spotted him busting her. "I guess you were about to head home now? You're breaking curfew, Marley. I'm going to have to take you in."

"Sorry, but I'm here as a reporter. You can't cite me." She turned back to the building. "I'm doing my job."

He marched in her direction. "You can't wander the streets alone. The sheriff said both gangs are headed back to town." He slid his phone back into his pocket.

"I'll leave when it becomes too dangerous, but I have to take photos. I'd like one of the bikers congregating and maybe the moment they throw the first punch, but after that I'll be happy to go home."

"You are one stubborn woman." He released a heavy sigh. "Bear and I will be going with you." The sheriff had told him to watch over Marley long before he deputized him.

A truck slowed. The driver flashed his deputy badge. "She breaking curfew?"

"News reporter." Dirk smiled. "I'm escorting her. You pick anyone up?"

"Nah." He grinned. "I give 'em a warning. They're only curious. Stay safe. I overheard the sheriff say we might have to don riot gear if things get real bad."

Dirk glanced at Marley. "We'll hurry." He'd need to be at the office helping his fellow deputies, not tagging along while a pretty news reporter took pictures. He should've stuck to his instinct to take her to the station. If he knew Marley as he thought he did, she'd plow right into the danger before he could begin to convince her to go home.

"We'll go fast. I know you're needed elsewhere."

They headed to the left, following the street's curve back to Main Street. The area flickered with untreated blazes. The acrid air trembled with the roar of motorcycles. Too many of them.

"Wait." He shot an arm out to stop Marley. "Bear. Stay." Dirk slowly moved down the street.

The roars had stopped followed by an eerie silence, then the slap of a fist into leather, and the air filled with curses. Dirk swallowed past a dry throat. This was not going to be good.

"Just a couple of photos, I promise." Marley moved past him.

"Not too close." With Bear at his side, he followed her onto Main Street. The sheriff's department van sat half a block away from the T-Junction. "I need to get my gear. Take your photos, then back in the van. You'll be safer there than on the street."

She nodded and started snapping pictures.

Not wanting to leave her for long, even with Bear by her side, Dirk took a deep breath against the pain in his ribs and jogged to the van.

"Good. You're here. Get suited up." Sheriff Westbrook thrust riot gear at him. Wear the mask. We'll be tossing smoke grenades in hopes of breaking up the fight."

He put on the vest, helmet, and tool belt, then picked up his shield. "Are we all going in a united front?"

"First, we'll take up presence at the end of Oak and Main. If the fight accelerates to more than words, we toss the grenades. If it continues, we go in using force. Tasers only. No guns. Our jail will be overflowing tonight."

Dirk nodded and turned to join his fellow deputies, all looking the same as he did. Determination and a hint of fear shone in their eyes. He gripped his shield tighter. They formed a line across the street.

Borrowed law enforcement lined the other ends of the T. Bikers outnumbered law enforcement.

Dirk's palms started to sweat. His eyes darted to the sidewalk, then to the end of the street where he'd left Marley. She'd vanished.

Chapter Thirteen

Spotting the biker, Dave, on the other side of the road, Marley stepped off the curb and headed his way. At that moment, someone threw a rock and started a fight. Before she could turn back, angry, leather-wearing men surrounded her, intent on causing damage to someone. She was swept along in the tide.

No amount of pushing and shoving could free her. Fear clogged her throat. She'd wanted a firsthand account of the mob in order to write the article, but this was too close for her liking.

"Let me out!" She shoved against one large man and found herself pushed back in return. Where was law enforcement?

Someone stepped on her foot. Another elbowed her in the ribs as he drew his fist back to throw a punch.

Marley ducked and did her best to escape by going under arms and around fighting bodies. Not an easy task when everyone around her outweighed her by at least eighty pounds. By the time she broke free, she emerged on the opposite end of where she'd started.

There was no way across other than back through

the mob. She'd have to find another way to reach the sheriff's van.

She scanned up and down the sidewalk. More men were arriving to join the fray. Men in coveralls and jeans. Farmers, not bikers. The visiting bikers were in a fight they couldn't win. But why, when it was one of theirs that had been brutally murdered?

"May I ask you a question?" She stopped a middle-aged man. "Why get involved? It wasn't one of Misty Hollow's residents who died."

"To run off the riffraff and save our town." He frowned. "We vowed when that crime boss was here that we wouldn't allow that kind of thing here again. They're accusing our people of murder, ma'am. Those are Misty Hollow Angels. They protect us, so we, in turn, protect them. Excuse me." He stepped off the curb and joined in the fight.

Marley turned in the direction of the van only to find her way blocked by more arriving town residents. This wasn't a fight; this was a slaughter. She snapped a couple of photos and tried pushing her way through, much like a salmon fighting to go upstream.

The crowd fought against her. She turned right to enter an alley. If she made it out the other end, she might be free. After the noise of the fight, the alley seemed eerily quiet. The hair on her arms stood on end. Instinct told her to flee. She turned to run.

A man in leather blocked her way. She tilted her head up to try and make out his features. With his back to the light, she couldn't see anything. He reached for her. She whipped around, evading his grasp, and sprinted down the alley.

Pounding footsteps let her know he gave chase and

was quickly gaining on her. She knocked over some cardboard boxes stacked against a dumpster, tossed a bag of garbage his way, and kept running. She screamed and tried to divert her path when someone else stepped out in front of her holding an iron bar. She took a couple of steps back before recognizing Jane. "We have to go fast." She tried dragging Jane away.

Jane brandished the bar like a baseball bat. "Back away, man. I ain't afraid to use this. You can't go accosting women in this town."

The man laughed. "Who's going to stop me? You and that pretty little thing?"

"Yes." Jane stepped in front of Marley.

"Let's go. We can tell the sheriff's department about him."

Jane shook her head. "He'll get away. Scum like him doesn't deserve to live." She swung the bar.

The man deflected it with his arm and howled as it connected with bone. "I'm going to kill you."

"I'd like to see you try."

"Jane. Please." Marley kept tugging until she reluctantly started to back up.

Once they were free of the alley and within sight of the van, Marley faced the woman. "What are you doing here? I thought you said you were headed home."

"I was, but I couldn't get there because of the crowded streets. I tried to find a way around when I ran into you and that thug." She slapped the bar against her palm. "You should've let me deal with him."

Who was this woman? "We aren't here to fight. Come on. I told Dirk I'd wait for him at the sheriff's van. I suggest you drop the bar before they think you're a threat."

Jane tossed it under a bush. "I'm going home. This way is clear enough."

"Thank you, friend." Marley smiled and headed for the van.

~

Annie skirted around to the next street, then back to retrieve the iron bar. With it in hand, she returned to the alley in hopes of finding the man who tried to harm Marley. She would never again lose someone she cared about because of the actions of another.

She found him leaning against a dumpster drinking whiskey from a paper bag. That explained his foolishness in trying to attack Marley.

Seeing Annie, he pushed away from the dumpster and tossed the bottle on the ground. "You again? Sorry, lady, you don't interest me."

"You interest me. Why aren't you out there fighting instead of chasing defenseless women?"

"No taste for fighting." He grinned, revealing a gold tooth. "I do have a taste for pretty ladies, though. Wandering around this late by herself is an invitation in my book."

Annie would make him pay for those words. First, she'd knock out his teeth, taking the gold one as a souvenir. "That woman happens to be my friend. I don't like it when people try to harm her." She took a step forward, her fingers wrapped tight around the bar.

The man laughed and moved forward to meet her. "Let's dance."

She raised the bar and swung it at his face.

~

Shoulder to shoulder, Dirk and the other deputies moved forward, holding their shields in front of them.

What he should be doing was look for Marley. Anything could've happened to her with this mob.

"Wilbur, go home." He shouted at an older man who was a regular at the diner. "Same for your friends. Don't make me arrest you." They had no room for all these men in the jail. The best they could hope for was to run them off. He held up a smoke grenade. "You have two minutes to spread the word."

Wilbur scowled, then shouted that smoke grenades were going to be launched. Most of the men that weren't bikers started to disperse. Good. They didn't need well-meaning vigilantes to get in the way of law enforcement.

"On three," the sheriff called out. "One, two, launch."

Dirk pulled his mask into place and released his grenade. The road filled with smoke and shouting. He struggled to see through the smoke. Most men seemed to be coughing and pulling bandanas over their mouth and nose, while others still struggled to throw punches.

The line of deputies moved forward cutting through the mob. Dirk stumbled when someone shoved him from the back, but he managed to stay on his feet. He turned and lifted his club, lowering his hand when he recognized Dave.

"Go home before you're arrested."

The big man shook his head. "Sorry. Can't. We've a reputation to uphold." The man's knees buckled.

Behind him, a man held a bloody knife. He came at Dirk.

Dirk pulled his weapon and shot him. Blood splattered his shield.

The sound of the shot echoed, freezing men in their

tracks. Dirk raised his gun to the sky. "Disperse and go home or be arrested." He turned to the sheriff. "I need help here." Then he knelt next to Dave. "Where did he get you?"

"The upper arm. I'll be okay."

"Lean on me. I'll move you clear of this." Dirk shoved his shoulder under the man's good arm and helped him to the sidewalk. "Give me the bandana around your face."

"I'll choke."

"It's that or bleed to death."

Dave turned so Dirk could untie the cloth. He tied the bandana as tight as he could. "Stay put. I'll send a medic over here." Dirk spoke into his radio.

By now, some of the crowd had filtered away, leaving only the injured and those refusing to back down. Still too many for the jail, but they'd have to be crowded in.

Dirk helped round them up, dividing the two gangs. He'd never met so many idiots in his life. Save their reputation? A man had been murdered. They ought to be working together to find the killer, not trying to kill each other.

One of the men darted toward the alley. Dirk motioned to the sheriff that he'd give chase, then followed, shouting for the man to stop.

He didn't spare Dirk a glance.

When Dirk rounded the corner, the man stood next to a body. He whirled, hands up. "I didn't do it, I swear."

"Against the wall. Keep your hands up." Dirk moved to the body, raised his shield, and removed his mask to get a better look. He radioed the sheriff.

The victim lay in a pool of blood, his face beaten unrecognizable. Teeth lay scattered across his chest like popcorn.

The sheriff arrived. "That the killer?"

"I don't think so. I chased him in here. This guy was already lying on the ground. I'll look around for a murder weapon."

"Can I go now?" The man who'd stumbled across the body started to lower his hands.

"No. You're under arrest for participating in the riot." He shined his flashlight back and forth as he moved slowly down the alley. The streetlight near the dumpster had a broken bulb, leaving the area in darkness. At the dumpster, he peered inside, moving some bags and boxes out of the way. There. A bloody iron bar. "Sheriff."

Westbrook peered into the dumpster. "I'll get the crime scene over here. It's going to be a long night."

Dirk agreed. He stepped to the side and sent Marley a text. "Are you okay? I'm going to be busy for a few hours yet."

She replied instantly. "That's okay. I'm at the van, but I'm going to head home. The house isn't damaged on the inside. All the locks and safety measures still work. I'll see you at the diner for breakfast?"

"Yes." The worry over her slid off his back.

The sheriff wiped his forehead. "I'll take this guy back to the street. We're going to start booking them out there. See how many we have not going to the hospital. Can you handle this? Crime scene should be here within the hour."

Dirk nodded and waited in the alley for the crime team while the sheriff escorted the other man back. He leaned against the building and stared at the body. Why beat the man to death here? The fight was in the street. Had someone lured him here?

He pushed away from the wall and studied the area around him for clues. One partial bloody footprint near the dumpster. Not a large shoe. Small like a woman's? Could a woman do this to a man his size? He glanced over his shoulder at the body. The victim wasn't a small man. It would take a lot of strength to do this. Or rage.

This death seemed very similar to the death at the motel. The same killer? Which group did this man belong to? He wasn't one of the Misty Angels, but that didn't mean he wasn't one of their guests. Then again, he could be from the same group as the other dead man. Too many questions and not enough answers.

He sighed and removed his helmet, welcoming the slight breeze cooling the perspiration plastering his hair to his skull. A can rattled down the alley. He froze, peering through the darkness.

Was that someone moving? He pulled his gun and continued to stare in that direction. The shadow moved again.

"Who's there?" He suddenly felt very much alone.

A cat yowled and darted across his path. The shadow remained where he'd spotted it. A trick of the light, maybe.

"Deputy?"

He turned as three men wearing crime-scene jackets approached. He glanced back to find the shadow gone.

Chapter Fourteen

Drat! Annie rushed back to the motel. She'd almost gotten rid of the farmer. It had been the perfect setting. The sheriff would've thought he was killed by the same person who killed the biker. But she'd waited too long to make a move and lost the opportunity. Now she'd have to wait for another one to come.

Bolting the door behind her, she turned on the shower. Now she'd have to burn her clothes. No amount of laundry detergent would erase the blood, so burning was the only way to destroy the evidence.

After adjusting the water to a comfortable but hot temperature, she stepped under the spray. The water that ran off her body turned red, then pink, then clear. The brutal murder of the biker had been gory, but the man deserved every strike of the bar. How dare he assault Marley?

She closed her eyes and leaned her forehead against the cool tile of the shower wall. Her daughter Lauren hadn't gone swimming that fateful day. She'd been taken to the lake against her will, raped, murdered, and dumped. No way would Annie let the same thing happen to Marley. If she could've killed the man who had taken her baby, she would have and smiled while doing it.

After her shower, she collapsed on the bed, not bothering to get dressed. Sheer exhaustion put her to sleep almost as soon as her head hit the pillow.

~

Marley waved as a very tired-looking Dirk entered the diner. "Did you go home at all?"

"A couple of hours ago." He slid in the booth across from her. "It took a long time to book all those men. Not to mention the murder in the alley. That took most of my time, since I found the body."

"Alley?" She shuddered thinking of her near escape. "A man tried to attack me on my way to the van."

His eyes flashed. "What?"

"I'll tell you later." She pasted on a smile as Jane headed their way. "Good morning."

"Good morning." She sat next to Marley without being invited. "I need coffee and lots of it. The bikers made so much noise getting to their rooms I barely got any sleep."

Marley frowned. "You live at the motel?" She assumed Jane lived near her after all the times she'd mentioned passing her house on her way home.

"Sure. It's very convenient since I work there." She looked at Marley as if she'd grown a second nose. "Why? Is there something wrong with that?"

"No." She focused on the coffee in front of her as their server filled cups for Dirk and Jane. Maybe Jane had told her that she did, and she'd forgotten. "Is the danger over, Dirk?"

"Between the two groups? Yeah. Too many injuries for them to be happy about the fighting. When we were able to get Dave and Ben—that's the other leader—to sit and actually talk things out, they realized that whoever killed that man in the motel wasn't one of them." He chuckled. "Wasn't hard to get them to talk since they were both in the same room at the ER. Sheriff Westbrook told me that he'd handcuffed them to their beds so they didn't have any other option but to talk."

"Smart man." She smiled. "I started writing the article this morning. My old boss and the local paper are interested."

"Will you be able to make a living doing freelance?"

"I think so."

His grin widened. "Does that mean you're going to stay in Misty Hollow?"

"Yeah. I'm already considering my living options once my lease is up. The landlord is having the porch repaired today, so I'll spend most of my time here writing or at the coffee shop." Nothing like construction noise to keep a writer from writing. "I'd come to this town to hide, but I found a place to stay instead."

Jane had stayed quiet while they talked but now interrupted. "That's great news."

The tone of her voice didn't match her words. Instead, she sounded as if she had to force the words from her throat. Why would Jane care whether Marley stayed or not? They'd just…She widened her eyes. The woman needed to leave so she could talk to Dirk in private.

But she didn't. Instead, Jane ordered breakfast to

go. "A future author and a news reporter. And to think that a person of your stature is friends with little ole me."

Dirk shot her a quick look, then shrugged in Marley's direction. "She's also friends with a rice farmer. Seems our local celebrity has her feet firmly planted on the ground."

Marley changed the subject before Jane got too gushy. "How's the progress on the tiny houses coming?"

"Ready to start assembling the kits." He straightened as their server brought his omelet. "I won't be doing much today, though. This boy will be catching up on his sleep."

Jane slid from the booth, scooping the Styrofoam container that held her order. "I need to get to work. See you around." She rushed from the building.

"What's up with her?" Dirk shook his head.

The server removed Jane's mug and carried it to the kitchen.

"This might seem like a strange question, but…how was the man in the alley killed?" Her mouth dried up at her suspicion.

"With an iron bar. Why?"

"When I was running from the man in the alley, Jane found us. I had to drag her away because she wanted to start a fight. Dirk, she was carrying an iron bar."

~

"Wow. I think we may have found Annie." His blood chilled. The woman was around Marley a lot. Too much.

Marley nodded. "She's always there when I'm in

trouble. She tried to save me from the house when she thought it was burning. The dead man at the motel must've been the one who accidentally punched me. Then, the one in the alley." Marley wrapped her arms around herself. "She kills whoever she thinks has hurt me. I'm the reason those men are dead."

"Stop thinking that way." He reached across the table and took her hand. "Annie killed those men. Not you, but I need to let the sheriff know." He stood. "Don't let on that we suspect her. Keep playing the game. If she knows we're on to her, she could snap. Try to get something with her fingerprints if you can." He glanced at the swinging door of the kitchen.

They'd had her prints right in front of them. If only they'd known to grab the mug before the server did. "We can compare them to the ones found on the bar."

"It shouldn't be too difficult. I let her know I'd be here or at the coffee bar. I guarantee you that I'll see her at noon." She slid from the booth, her face pale. "I have to admit that I'm terrified. Dirk, I'm not an actor. What if she realizes we know?"

"Work hard at keeping her from doing that." He cupped her cheek. "Once I tell the sheriff, he'll send a deputy to bring her in for questioning. Getting her fingerprints will seal her fate. Don't go anywhere there aren't a lot of people, okay?"

She leaned into his touch. "I won't."

He wanted to stay, to hug her close, shelter her. But Annie needed to be stopped. The sheriff had to know. Then, Dirk would meet up with Marley and never leave her side until the other woman was behind bars. "I'll join you later."

Reluctant to leave her, he pulled away and rushed

to his truck. A few minutes later, he sat across from the sheriff.

Sheriff Westbrook rubbed his eyebrow. "This whole case is giving me a twitch." He sighed. "Sure sounds as if this Jane might be Annie. I'll have her brought in."

"Marley thinks she'll show up wherever she is at noon. She mentioned being at either the diner or the coffee shop."

"Good. That'll be easier." He offered his hand for a shake. "If you ever get tired of farming, I could use a man like you as a full-time deputy."

Dirk returned the handshake. "I think I'd rather be a temporary one when the need arises. Now that I have big plans for my farm."

"You're doing a good thing. Stay close to Miss Brooks until this is over, which shouldn't be long now."

"Sure will." He'd go home, grab a couple of hours of sleep, then find a place to watch over Marley without Jane/Annie seeing him. No way would he allow Marley to confront the woman without him somewhere close by. Finding out how physically close her stalker was would leave Marley shaken and needing comfort. Something he was more than glad to give.

Back at the farm, he crashed into bed with Bear snoring from his bed on the floor and didn't wake for two hours, which left him with some time to check out the building site. Then, he could work more on turning the barn into a training center.

The builders worked quickly. One house was ready for the roof. At this rate, Dirk could start bringing folks in soon. He'd pay a visit to the homeless out by the lake tonight and see how many veterans were interested in living and working on the farm.

Seeing everything was under control at the houses, he headed for the barn. Bear sat in the door as if on guard. Not for the first time, he contemplated leaving the dog with Marley. He had Duke and Luke. Speaking of…the two hadn't greeted him when he'd arrived home earlier.

"Come on, boy. Find the dogs." He snapped his fingers for Bear to start tracking.

They stopped back at the building site. "Sure, I saw the two of them race into the woods a few hours ago. Don't know if they came back," one of the builders said.

"Thanks." He followed Bear into the trees.

At maybe the length of a football field from the tiny houses, he spotted the dogs on the ground with ropes around their necks. The rise and fall of their bellies showed they were alive. Someone had drugged them. Someone who wanted to get closer to Dirk.

A twig snapped behind him.

He whirled.

Bear's hackles raised. He growled deep in his throat.

Dirk should've brought his gun was the last thought he had as Annie shrieked and leaped from behind a tree to slam a thick stick against his head. Dirk dropped to his knees as Bear lunged at her. Annie screamed again, bashed the dog across the rib cage, and then sprinted away.

"Bear." Dirk used a nearby tree to help him struggle to his feet. "Stay." No way he'd risk the dog's life. He untied the other two so they could make their way home when they woke up. Dirk took slow steps back down the path.

He put fingers to the side of his head, relieved to find them dry. A knot had formed but no blood. Nothing a couple of aspirin wouldn't take care of. "Good boy. You okay? She didn't hurt you, did she?" Because he'd strangle her if she did. He ran his hands over the dog, not finding anything broken.

Back at the barn, he called the sheriff and filled him in on the latest. "I'm not sure now whether she'll show up to meet Marley."

"We'll find her," the sheriff said.

Unless she hid up in the mountain. That could take a while. He glanced in that direction. A lot of folks had tried to hide up there. They were all eventually found, but it had taken longer. He wanted this whole thing stopped so he could see whether he had a future with Marley or not.

He turned back to the barn. What did Annie want to do that she had to get rid of the dogs? Get to him? Most likely. But, she had to know that Bear never left Dirk's side while the man was on the farm.

Unless she'd planned on taking care of them both at once.

Chapter Fifteen

Marley wiped her sweaty palms on a napkin for what had to be the tenth time. Where was Annie? It was fifteen past twelve.

The last day's events would add multiple chapters to her book. She was ready to see the end.

She stared through the large shop window at what had once been a vacant video store now burned to the ground. A few other businesses—the flower shop, a woman's boutique—hadn't been vacant. The owners had lost everything.

Thankfully, no residents had been killed. A few had been injured—people who shouldn't have been at the fight to begin with—but no deaths other than the man in the alley. Businesses could be rebuilt.

Annie burst through the door, her gaze searching the shop. She smiled when she found Marley. "Sorry, I'm late. I was running late getting a room ready for a new guest." She plopped into a chair.

The barista set a coffee in front of her. Annie's eyes widened. "You ordered for me?"

"Sure. I've seen how you like your coffee at the

diner. I asked them to bring this when you arrived."

She reached across the table and put her hand on Marley's. "You are the best friend a girl could have."

Marley fought not to show revulsion at the woman's touch. Those hands had brutally killed at least two men.

"How did you sleep?" Annie blew on her coffee.

"Not long enough. I'm hoping to take a nap this afternoon." Marley watched as the other woman set her cup on the table. Hopefully, Annie wouldn't stay long, and Marley could get her cup for fingerprints.

"Bad thing last night." Annie shook her head. Her acting skills deserved an Academy Award. Tears even brimmed in her eyes. "I had nightmares." She dabbed at them with a napkin.

Marley made a noncommittal sound in her throat. The woman didn't need to have nightmares; she was a walking, talking example of one. "You have leaves in your hair." Strange if she came from work.

"Oh, thank you." She patted her head, removing the leaves and dropping them on the table. "How are the repairs on your place coming along?"

"Finished." Marley forced a smile. "Pays to have money, I guess."

"I wouldn't know. All I have is my disability and what I make at the motel." Her eyes widened and she clapped a hand over her mouth. "Oops. Don't let disability find out I'm working."

"Your secret is safe with me." Where was the deputy? She didn't know how long she could keep the woman here.

"Found a place to stay on a more permanent basis yet?"

"I'm thinking about buying a plot of land and building a tiny house. I wanted to go look at some today, but I'm too tired."

Annie's grin widened. "I'd love to go with you. It might be something I'd want to do when I tire of the motel. Let's go tomorrow."

"Sounds good." Hopefully, by tomorrow, Annie would already be in a tiny house at the sheriff's. A jail cell.

"Excuse me. I need to use the little girl's room." Annie, a trail of dirt from her shoes following her, headed for the restroom, but there sat her near-empty coffee cup.

Marley emptied the coffee into her drink and dropped the cup into her bag. She sent a quick text to Dirk. "Where is the deputy?"

"No idea. I'm at the farm. Annie attacked me in the woods. Be careful. I'll contact the sheriff."

She hung up. Annie had attacked Dirk? Marley wanted to confront her, but that would set her off, maybe harming someone or worse.

When Annie returned, Marley did her best to paste a pleasant look on her face and not show the fear that chilled her. "You were finished, weren't you? I let the barista take your cup."

"Yeah, I have things to do. See you about this time tomorrow morning to go tiny-house shopping?"

"Sure, Ann...Jane."

Annie's eyes narrowed. "You set me up."

"I don't know what you're talking about." Her heart stuttered.

"You know who I am."

"Well, yes." She forced a smile. "Annie and Jane

had too many similarities. I am a news reporter, remember? I simply put two-and-two together. No more need for secrecy."

She heaved a sigh. "That's good. It's too difficult to keep such a thing going. What a relief." She flashed a grin and strode from the coffee shop.

Marley sagged in her chair and sent a text to Dirk letting him know she'd messed up.

~

Wow. If Annie had known how well Marley would accept knowing who she was, she'd have stopped the silly letters a long time ago. Maybe it was this place. Misty Hollow was different from the big city. Marley wasn't near as busy, and Annie wasn't living in a cardboard palace. The friendship had time to grow and be nurtured.

When she reached the motel fifteen minutes later, she caught blinking red and blue lights speeding in the same direction. Annie stepped into the bushes near the parking lot and hunkered down.

Two deputies exited the car and headed for the manager's office. A few minutes later, they approached her room.

Her blood boiled. Marley had betrayed her. She gritted her teeth so hard her jaw ached. Now, she had nothing. No place to stay, no job, and no friend. Everything she owned was in that room. She'd have to find a place to hide for a while and return at nightfall.

It had all been a ploy, and they would all have to pay. Staying to the trees lining the road, she made her way to the highway and hitchhiked a ride to the lake and the homeless community. She'd familiarize herself with the area until it grew dark.

Finding the last unoccupied section among the other tents and cardboard houses, she took a stick and wrote *taken* in the dirt. Straightening, she studied the people sitting outside their homes. Mostly men. A couple of women sat with vacant stares on their faces.

Annie stuck her hand in her pocket and took comfort from feeling the knife she always kept on her. Anyone who tried to bother her would regret their actions. With Marley's betrayal came distrust and fury. Annie wouldn't let anyone get close. Ever.

Her rage hadn't diminished by nightfall. She returned to the motel and laughed at the deadbolt that had been placed on her room door. There were bolt cutters in the supply room.

Knife in hand, she paid a visit to the manager first. Anyone who had a hand in Marley's betrayal would die. Even for something as simple as showing the authorities which room was Annie's?

It didn't take long for her to break in and start tossing her belongings out the bathroom window. She took everything, including the bedding and towels. Taking the extra blanket out of the closet, she tied everything inside and grunted as she hefted it onto her shoulder. She'd be comfortable enough that night, but tomorrow she would need to find a box. Time to build another palace while she plotted her revenge.

The hour grew late, and the full moon hung high in the sky by the time she returned to the lake. She curled up in the motel comforter and slept.

~

His heart had dropped to his knees at Marley's text. Now, he strode toward her car and pulled her into his arms the moment she got out. "How did she act?"

"Very well. I acted as if I'd known sooner. She seemed pleased. Did the deputy pick her up?"

"No sign of her at the motel. They waited several hours." He put his arm around her shoulders and escorted her to the porch. "Looks like she doesn't trust you after all. Fingerprints?"

"I dropped the cup she used off at the sheriff's office." She lowered into an Adirondack chair.

"I'll get some tea." Dirk went to the kitchen and poured two tall glasses. It might be getting late, but he had a feeling neither of them could sleep right now.

He was wrong. Soft snores came from a sleeping Marley. He set the glasses down and scooped her into his arms. "Come on, sweetheart." Inside, he laid her on the sofa, removed her shoes, and then covered her up with a throw. Bear lay under the coffee table, his eyes on Marley.

Not wanting her out of his sight while Annie was on the loose, Dirk leaned back in his recliner. It didn't take long for his eyes to grow heavy.

He woke six hours later. Seeing that Marley still slept, he got quietly out of the chair and headed for the kitchen to fix breakfast and start the coffee. Marley joined him a few minutes later.

"Did I wake you?" He handed her a cup of coffee.

"No, the delicious aroma of java did." She smiled. "Thanks for letting me crash."

"Until Annie is caught, I think you should stay here where I can help keep you safe."

"My rental is the safest place to be."

"Then Bear and I will come there."

Her eyes flashed before she nodded. "Okay. I've plenty of room. What about the farm?"

"We'll come here during the day. I can't let my work slide." He leaned against the counter and sipped his drink. "You can write here as well as anywhere."

"The coffee shop is always full of people."

Why was she so reluctant to stay at the farm? He understood her house was a fortress, but he also knew she couldn't stay in it twenty-four hours a day.

She set her cup firmly on the counter. "I don't want to be mean, Dirk, but the guard dogs were poisoned, and you were hit over the head. That doesn't sound safe to me."

She made a good point. "Okay, but I want hourly texts so I know you're fine. Don't go anywhere alone. I'll meet up with you as soon as I can. You hungry?"

"Yes, thank you." She sat at the kitchen table and patted Bear's ears. "You keep your human safe, okay? Your buddies aren't doing such a good job."

Dirk shook his head. "Trained guard dogs should know not to take food from someone they don't know. I'm returning them today."

"Maybe they didn't eat anything. Maybe she gave them a shot. I wouldn't put anything past her." She glanced over her shoulder. "You never used to close the blinds."

"That was before she snuck up on me. I won't let it happen again." He cracked eggs into a bowl. "The woman must have some kind of training. She's like a ghost."

"Once we match her fingerprints, we can dig deeper. Maybe she's former military."

He stiffened and faced her. "Why didn't I think about that possibility? That would explain her skill at fighting and sneaking through the woods." Being former military police, he should've thought of that. Was his worry over Marley affecting his senses? Were his feelings for her clouding his ability to make wise judgments? Yes. He'd never been in charge of keeping a woman safe before, and he had let his caring for her confuse him.

He stared at the woman nursing her coffee. How much danger had he put her in by letting his emotions take over? The smart thing to do would be to take a step back. Treat her as the job the sheriff asked him to do.

When and only when the danger was past would he allow himself to explore a relationship with her.

"I told Annie I was going to be looking at tiny houses today. I doubt she'll be there since I blew her cover."

"If you do go, she'll be there, but not where you can see her." He took a sharp breath through his nose. "She'll be lying in wait."

Chapter Sixteen

Annie taped several large boxes together, dividing her castle into rooms, and made the place a home. Never should she have left her last one and come to Misty Hollow. She'd been happy, at least sort of. Until she'd wanted to be Marley's friend.

She started blowing up a single-wide air mattress. The deceitful woman reminded Annie so much of Lauren. Well, like her daughter, Marley was dead to her. Soon, she'd be truly dead just like that author.

It panged her heart a bit. She'd become closer to Marley than to anyone.

Bed blown up and bedding in place, she crawled from her new home. Time to create some havoc on the farm. She might as well have a little fun before things intensified.

She'd managed to make the other homeless people believe her insane, and they gave her a wide berth as she moved between the tents and boxes. All it had taken to convince them of her insanity was to wield her knife and look deranged.

Laughing, she acted like she was going to lunge at

an old man which sent him scurrying for cover. She liked scaring them. Soon, Marley and the farmer would also be afraid.

Before going to the farm, Annie visited a cow rancher and disguised her scent with manure. Maybe she was a bit crazy.

~

Marley washed their plates from lunch. She'd give Dirk one day of her staying on the farm, but she had a job to do, articles to write, reporting to scoop out, and a book to write. She glanced out the window. "Dirk?"

"Yeah?" He glanced up from a ledger he jotted numbers into.

"Did you leave a light on in the barn?"

"I don't think so." He closed the ledger and rose to his feet. "I'll go check." He opened the back door and whistled for Duke and Luke. "Come on, Bear."

"I'm coming with you." Someone needed to watch his back. She wasn't the only one in danger.

Dirk shook his head and grabbed his handgun from the counter. "I wish you'd listen."

"Remember we said we would watch out for each other." She hitched her chin. "It's probably nothing. You left the light on is all."

"Right." He didn't look convinced. "Then stay behind me."

"Sure." Because harm never came at a person from behind.

The presence of the three dogs dispelled some of her fear. Annie couldn't sneak up on them with the dogs close by.

Dirk slid the barn door open. The main overhead light lit up the cavernous space now devoid of stalls and waiting to be transformed into a training facility. She'd be one of the first to sign up.

"Where's the light switch?"

"It's motion sensored. Anything bigger than Bear would set it off."

A human. "Wouldn't the horses have turned the light on?"

"There haven't been horses on this farm for years. I used the building for storage." He marched to the back door.

Duke and Luke set up barking as they tore from the barn.

Marley turned. Flames licked at the deck of the house. "Fire!" She grabbed a horse blanket from a pile near the door and darted for the house, Dirk passing her.

He grabbed the hose, turned on the faucet, then directed the stream toward the flame. It wasn't large, so it couldn't have burned more than a minute.

Marley stuck her blanket under the hose, then beat at the flames. Was Annie standing somewhere watching, or had she set the fire and fled? Marley wanted to beat her with the wet blanket.

The dogs tore past, again barking with frenzy. Marley shot Dirk a startled glance. "The barn."

They fought the fire at the house, then raced for the barn. "I've called the sheriff. Hopefully, we can get some help out here."

"Look." She pointed in the direction of the tiny houses. An orange glow rose in the sky.

"Not those." Dirk glanced at the barn, then back where the tiny house glowed in the distance. "At least I only had one built."

She put a hand on his arm. "I'm so sorry." He pulled away, a gesture that ripped at her heart. He'd never reacted to her touch like that before.

"Insurance will cover the cost." He turned on the hose connected to the barn and quickly doused the fire burning the edges of a fence post. "Keep a lookout. I want to know where she goes next."

Marley nodded. Other than the house, barn, and tiny houses, there wasn't anything left to burn. She doubted Annie would double around and hit the house again. Not when Duke and Luke searched the area. No, she'd torched the tiny house on her way into the woods.

Once the fire was out at the barn, they drove a side-by-side to the tiny house property. The one house had burned to the point beyond saving.

Dirk's shoulders slumped. "This makes me wonder whether I should halt production until Annie is caught."

"That might be best. You could visit the homeless community and see whether there's any interest. I can write an article for the paper to help spread the word about it coming in the future."

"That would be good."

They sat and watched the building burn until only the plumbing and the concrete slab the house had sat on remained. Heaving a sigh, Dirk drove them back to the house where the sheriff waited on the porch.

While Dirk told Sheriff Westbrook about the fires, Marley stared into the trees. Duke and Luke had returned and lay under the back deck.

Annie truly was a ghost. The dogs couldn't catch her, and she'd managed to travel from structure to structure without being caught. Which could only mean something she'd done to herself kept the dogs confused.

Her eyes widened as Annie stepped from the trees. The woman didn't smile or wave, simply stared. A brown substance covered her face and hands. The same substance coated her clothes.

"Dirk? Sheriff? She's here."

~

Dirk moved to Marley's side. He stared across the rice field to where Annie stood as still as one of the trees.

When the sheriff headed her way, she took off like a shot back into the trees. "I'll have regular patrols come out this way. I've already had them watching Miss Brooks's house."

"They need to patrol the woods. She won't approach from the road." Dirk pounded his fist on his thigh. The woman was a boil on his rear. "Why hasn't she been caught?"

"You'll understand a bit more once I tell you about the fingerprints."

"Have a seat on the porch." Curiosity burned through Dirk. "They came back fast."

"High-profile case." The sheriff sat. "The fingerprints belong to an Annie Wilson. The same Annie we're dealing with. She's ex-military, medically discharged after suffering a mental breakdown when her only child, a daughter, was brutally murdered while Annie was deployed. She did a short stint undercover in the Middle East."

Dirk's heart broke.

Tears poured down Marley's face. "That is so sad. No wonder she's the way she is."

"The woman is dangerous. She's skilled in fighting, tracking, and disappearing. That's what makes her so difficult to catch." The sheriff stood. "Now that we know more, we've taken a step forward. We'll nab her. The two of you need to be extremely careful."

The woman probably had more training than Dirk did. Keeping Marley safe had just become a lot harder. "We will." He actually considered staying with Marley in her house but quickly rejected the thought. He needed to be on the farm. "I'm going to hire a security guard to watch over the tiny houses." Dirk straightened his shoulders. I'm not going to stop production."

"Okay. We've a few we recommend. Give the office a call." The sheriff glanced from him to Marley. "Be careful, ma'am."

Dirk watched the sheriff drive away, then returned to his ledger. Number crunching was never his favorite part of the job. Another reason the tiny houses needed to move forward. Dirk needed the income the studio would provide which meant he needed people to work the farm.

"I need to go home." Marley hovered in the kitchen doorway. "Thanks again for letting me crash on the sofa."

"Any time." He barely looked up. "Text me when you arrive home and before you go anywhere else. I want to know where you are at all times."

"Oookay." She hesitated for a second, then left without saying goodbye.

He hated being standoffish, but he couldn't protect her and the ranch effectively if she occupied all his thoughts. He'd finish his work on the farm as quickly as possible, then meet her at the diner until she was ready to stay home for the night.

Once he'd finished the books, he called the

sheriff's office to get a number for a security guard, then the tiny house builder who said they had two units ready for assembly and would bring them over in the morning.

Since it wasn't rice-farming season, Dirk finished by eleven-thirty and sent Marley a text that he was heading to the diner. He'd been so busy trying to make the numbers work that he didn't realize she hadn't texted.

When she didn't return his recent text, he called her. "Where are you?"

"Sorry. I'm not home yet. I've had a flat and left the phone in the car while I tried to flag down a ride. This is a very lonely road." She gave him directions to her location.

"Be right there. Stay in the car." He snatched his keys from the small table near the front door, called Bear to come, and sprinted for his truck.

Guilt washed over him as he sped from the driveway. Marley had been on the road alone for two hours. Why hadn't she tried calling?

Using his Bluetooth, he tried to call her again, but the call went straight to voicemail. Now worry added to the guilt.

He pulled up behind her car and jumped out of his truck. The instant his boots hit the ground, Marley's door flew open, and she launched herself into his arms. So much for keeping his distance.

He wrapped her in a hug. "You okay?" He held her at arm's length and held her gaze.

"Yes. Just spooked because of the morning."

"I can understand that. Wait here by the truck with Bear while I put your spare on and follow you to the mechanic." He took his tools from the truck bed and approached the car. After retrieving the spare from the trunk, he jacked up the car and removed the tire. He rolled the tire toward his truck bed.

"Dirk!" He whirled.

A car sped directly toward him. He dove into the ditch. A loud shrieking sent birds shooting out of the trees.

Dirk scrambled to his feet as Marley and Bear exited the passenger side of the truck. "What happened?" He thought for sure the car had rammed his truck.

"It was Annie." Marley gripped his arms. "I saw her face as she scraped the side of the truck."

She must have waited for Dirk to arrive before showing her face. He'd also bet his favorite flannel shirt that she'd stolen that car from somewhere nearby.

"Did you run over something to get the flat?" He scanned the area.

"The tire started thumping a little ways back. I do remember running over something, but when I looked in the rearview mirror it looked like a stick."

Feeling as if Annie would come back to run him over again, he jogged up the road to find the stick. When he did, he picked it up. A line of long nails went in one end and out the other.

Annie had carefully planned the last few hours. This wouldn't stop her. She'd be back again, most likely raising the danger level.

He returned to the truck and showed Marley the stick. "I'll follow you to the mechanic."

"What are we going to do?" She frowned. "She's everywhere."

"I don't know, but I'm working on it." He had to figure out how to keep Annie from getting to Marley, and he had no idea how.

Chapter Seventeen

Marley woke the next morning restless. Despite top security in the house, her eyes had popped open at every little sound. Dirk had almost died the day before. He could easily have been run over. His tiny house had burned to the ground.

She knew that today he planned on visiting the homeless community, and she would be going with him. The drive to her house was too long for him to be alone, in her opinion. Anything could happen on the ten-mile drive.

Tossing aside the blankets, she padded to the shower, pausing only to view the security cameras of the night before. No sign of Annie, which was both a good and a bad thing. Good as far as not troubling Marley, but bad because if she remained in hiding, the authorities couldn't find her.

She waited at the front door for Dirk to arrive so her anxious heart could settle down. No matter how much she coaxed him, he refused to spend the nights in her safe haven. Stubborn man.

Finally. She opened the door before his truck

pulled up in her driveway.

"Anxious?" He smiled as she climbed in.

"Worried sick about you out there alone."

"Three dogs and a security guard." He backed away from the house. "That's not exactly alone."

"It didn't stop her from playing with matches, did it?" She hated driving to the diner when she lived within walking distance, but she wasn't foolish enough to go out alone. Not until Annie was behind bars. Since the woman had elevated the danger level, they had to increase the safety.

As soon as they were led to a booth, Lucy came to them. "This was dropped off for you, Marley."

She stared at the red envelope. No name on the front other than hers. "Who brought it?"

"I don't know. The hostess found it on her podium." She smiled and returned to the kitchen.

Sliding into the booth, Marley opened the envelope and pulled out a card. "It's a condolence card." She glanced at Dirk before reading the note. "*You're going to suffer the greatest loss. This could have been avoided. I will get to you.*" She dropped the card as if it burned her fingers.

"We'll drop the card off with the sheriff before going to the homeless community."

"I'm having second thoughts. What if Annie tries to attack both of us at once?"

"That's a given." He put his hand over hers. "I'm pretty sure that's her plan. I have what she couldn't get."

His touch stilled the tremors in her hands. "What's that?"

"Friendship," he said.

Her heart dropped. Had they really not progressed past the friendship stage? She sighed and read the board stating the day's special. Chicken fried steak and eggs. Heavy food to feed her heavy heart. "I'll have the special," she told the server.

Dirk ordered the same. "There's a strong possibility that Annie is staying with the homeless. By visiting there, we can find out for sure. I doubt we've had other female newcomers that might head in that direction."

"Then we should take a deputy with us."

"The men and women out there won't talk to us if we bring law enforcement. I'll keep my weapon on me."

Small consolation. Annie could shoot them sniper-style, and they wouldn't see it coming. Still, that would be preferable to the multiple knife wounds the poor author she'd killed had suffered.

They ate breakfast in silence. She figured Dirk's mind whirled as much as hers did over staying safe. He'd probably been in danger before as a military cop, but this was a first for her. If she'd known she'd attract a crazed stalker fan, she might have rethought her career choice.

After breakfast, they stopped by the sheriff's office to drop off the card. Sheriff Westbrook made a sound in his throat. "I really hope I'm the one to put cuffs on this woman. She's a thorn in my side for sure. I'm going to have a deputy follow you to the lake. He'll stay in his car, but I'll feel better knowing he's there as you drive around."

Marley felt better about the fact, too. No more nails in the road or attempts to run them over. "Thank you."

~

Annie wished she could've seen Marley's face when she received the card. It was fun taking her time, not killing her in a rage like she had the author. No, she enjoyed the torture. When it was time, because she reminded Annie of her daughter, she would make the woman's death swift.

Annie made her bed, then grabbed a towel and bar of soap. She'd found a spot among the cypress trees that gave her some privacy for bathing. It wouldn't work much longer, though, because the water was almost too cold. All she had to do was watch for snakes.

As Annie bathed then dressed in clean clothes so she could wash the dirty ones, she contemplated her next step. Eventually, she'd grow weary of the game. Was it time to plan how she'd nab Marley or wait until an opportunity presented itself? To do that, Annie would have to track her. She'd need a disguise so she wouldn't be seen.

No problem. She'd steal some men's clothes. If she wore them baggy and shoved her hair up under a ball cap, she wouldn't be immediately recognized. Not until it was too late. She'd like to get rid of the farmer, too, but he might have to wait. Marley was the one who'd betrayed her.

Annie carried her things home and put them away, hanging the wet towel and clothes on the clothesline she'd strung between two trees. Now for a cup of hot coffee to warm her after her bath. She set a metal cup on the small gas grill outside her door and poured water from a bottle. While the water boiled, she went inside to grab the instant coffee. Even a person living in a box could be civilized.

Before she'd taken her first sip, she heard a familiar voice. The farmer had arrived. Annie peeked around the corner of her house to see Marley with him. She scowled. There'd be no coffee. She went to the back of her home and sprinted for the trees, knowing she couldn't get to them with so many people around.

Always the planner, Annie had made sure to know where her avenue of escape would be and headed back to the lake. She'd swim across a narrow area and emerge behind a manufactured home where an old man lived. Then, she'd hot-wire his rusty old truck, steal some clothes, and find the next place to hide.

So much work. She splashed through the murky water, then swam when it became too deep. She'd return later for her things. If someone stole anything, she'd make sure they regretted it.

She entered through the trailer's back door, knife in hand. Thankfully for the man, he sat mouth agape snoring in a ratty recliner. Annie moved to the bedroom and stole the needed clothing, then snatched the truck keys from the man's nightstand. He never knew she was there.

Knowing there'd be a new manager at the motel since she'd rid the world of the last one, Annie parked the truck in the garage of an abandoned gas station/car repair. She changed her clothes, tugged her cap securely over her hair, and scurried head down to the motel office.

~

"Sure, we got lots of vets here. Some will be glad to work on the farm, but others are too riddled with drugs or alcohol to take you up on the offer." The man smoothed out his beard. "In fact, I'd be glad to give it a try, get my hands in the dirt. Rice farm, you say? Sure."

Dirk shook the man's hand and gave him a business card. "You get the first house. Should be ready next week. Could you point me to the next person who might join us?"

"Yeah, that patched-up army tent over yonder. Willy's a good sort."

The dream was quickly becoming a reality. With help, the studio would start making money as soon as he finished converting it. There wasn't a lot more work to do.

"You look like a child at Christmas." Marley slipped her hand in his.

"Nabbing my first resident is a bit like receiving a great gift." He gave her hand a squeeze. Once I've put the offer out here, I'll put an ad in the paper—let word of mouth find me others."

"You are going to do background checks, right?"

"I guess I'll have to." He glanced back to the man they'd just spoken to. "He seems all right. It doesn't matter if they have a criminal record because I believe in second chances. I just don't want addicts. The best way to tell is to talk to them." He'd always thought he had a good instinct about people until Annie. He never had a clue she was the one stalking Marley.

"Hello?" Dirk stopped in front of the army tent. "Your friend Ted sent me."

"What for?" A middle-aged man stepped from the tent. "Ain't nobody here real friends. What do you want?" He crossed his arms over stained, patched coveralls.

"I'm Dirk Mason. I own a rice farm down in the bottoms, and I'm looking for workers. In exchange for their work, I provide them with a home. Ted has agreed."

"You ain't paying anyone?" He frowned.

"No, sir, the house is payment. You'd be living alone in a 300 sq ft house equipped with all you need. There's no reason you can't work outside of the farm, but then you'd owe me three hundred in rent."

Willy tucked his tongue in his cheek. "Can I think on it? I mean, I got my disability and military retirement. Just never could get out of debt, so I chose not to have any living expenses. Even so, a hard roof would be better than a canvas one."

"Yes, sir." He handed him a card. "I'll have a house ready in two weeks. First come, first serve."

"Okay."

"One more question," Marley said. "Has there been anyone new arriving to the camp? A woman, maybe?"

"Yeah. She lives in that cardboard house with the curtains. Silliest thing I've ever seen. She calls it her palace." He jerked his chin down the line. "But she ain't here. I saw her run toward the lake a few minutes ago."

So close. "Thanks. I look forward to hearing from you. Anyone else that might be interested? It's for veterans only."

"Ruth who lives in that lean-to could use a roof over her head. Especially before winter. She's only got one leg though. Real leg anyway. Said she's here because she can't find a job that doesn't require a lot of standing. Prosthetic doesn't fit right."

"You can't turn away." Marley glanced in that direction. "Surely, there's something she could do."

She was right. He couldn't turn away a disabled anyone. He'd find her a way to earn her keep, maybe by cleaning the studio each evening he had clients. She could take as long as she needed. He'd also contact a buddy of his to get her the right-size prosthetic.

When he told Ruth about the tiny house and job, tears sprang to her eyes. "Do you realize that what you're doing will boost our confidence? Give us purpose? God bless you, young man." She clutched his hand in both of his. "I'd be glad to clean your studio even if it takes me all night."

By the time he and Marley reached Annie's cardboard home, he had five folks to live on his farm—six, if Willy decided to join them. They'd all be there within a month, moving in as each house was built.

"Wow." Marley peered in a window. "She really tried to make the place homey."

He opened the cardboard door, bent over, and stepped inside. "Three rooms." A bedroom, living room, and a dining room where the woman would have to sit Japanese style on the floor.

He had just started backing out when he stopped. "She'd been in the middle of making coffee." He pointed to the burnt cup, then reached down and turned off the propane. "Do you want me to take you home or to the farm after we let the deputy know she was here? We won't find her now. She's had an hour head start."

"Home. I want to do some writing." She cocked her head. "I promise not to leave the house."

He laughed. "Ah, since you promise." He took her hand. Forget keeping his distance. It had been a silly idea thinking he could stop caring about her at the drop of a hat. His worry might distract him at times, but they were in this together.

"The woman was here?" The deputy asked after joining. "Not many folks are willing to live like that."

"She's made herself pretty comfortable. I'm taking Marley home, then I'm heading to my farm."

He nodded. "I'll be right behind you until you reach the farm."

"A person has to know the homeless community is there. It's not a place someone would stumble upon accidentally. Not easily anyway." Marley clicked her seatbelt into place. "How did Annie know it was here? Does the homeless community communicate to each other where these places are?"

"Since quite a few of them are transients, I guess they do." He drove toward her house. "Annie most likely knew about the place before she arrived in Misty Hollow. Probably heard it from someone at the motel."

"What else does she know about this place?"

He'd be willing to bet she'd taken the time to familiarize herself with the town's layout, even the surrounding area. It made it easier for her to hide, move around, and stay out of reach. Dirk parked in front of Marley's house. Where are you, Annie?

Chapter Eighteen

Marley texted Dirk that she was going to go to the Misty Motel that morning and do a write-up on the murders that had occurred there. Her phone rang seconds after she pressed send.

"Absolutely not."

"It'll be fine, Dirk. A deputy is following me over. Annie won't be there."

"How do you know?"

"Why would she go back to where she lived and worked? The authorities would suspect that. They would have checked. I'm an investigative reporter. This is my job." Marley didn't want to defy him, but she would if he put his foot down. She already felt like a prisoner with an around-the-clock deputy patrol.

"If you're sure a deputy will be there."

"Positive. I made sure before I texted you. And, I need more material for my book."

"Meet me at the diner for lunch, okay?"

"Absolutely." She hung up and headed to the shower. With only a half an hour before the deputy arrived, breakfast would consist of toast and coffee.

By the time Deputy Johnson arrived, she was ready with her phone and notepad in her bag. She locked the house and set the alarm, then waved at the deputy and slid into her car. The deputy's presence did make her feel a lot safer.

She parked in front of the manager's office. Johnson pulled alongside her. She exited the car and motioned for him to lower his window. "I'm going to speak with the manager first, then visit both Annie's room and the one where the biker was killed. Can you give me that amount of time?"

"All the time you need. Reports to type." He motioned to his laptop. "I'm good."

She smiled and nodded, then pushed open the door to the manager's office. "Good morning. I'm Marley Brooks, reporter. Mind if I ask you a few questions about the recent activities going on here? It'll be good promo for the motel." Plenty of people liked to stay where a murder had taken place, something she'd never understand.

"I'm pretty new here, so I'm not sure how much I can tell you." The woman turned from her computer.

Marley glanced at the sign on the desk. "That's fine, Ms. Ramson. Whatever you can tell me will help. I'm sure you've heard things through the grapevine."

"That I have." She tsked and folded her hands on her desk. "A mad woman worked and lived here. Brutally killed several people. I'd like to say things like this don't happen in Misty Hollow, but this poor place has been besieged lately. Its remote location is an attraction for bad people looking for a place to hide."

The exact reason Marley had chosen the town. A lot of good that had done her. She hadn't thought for a second that her crazed fan would have put a tracker on her. "May I see the rooms?

"One has been cleaned, but sure." She handed her two key cards. "Don't mess anything up."

Promising not to, she headed to the room where the crime had taken place. The hair on her arm stood up as she unlocked the door. Places where violence had occurred, a violence that resulted in death, always made her antsy.

A made-up bed with a multi-colored, striped comforter dominated the room. A small table and chair, a kitchenette, a tiny bathroom. Nothing overly special except for a stain behind the bedpost someone had missed.

Marley imagined the man lying there, sleeping. He'd been tied to the headboard. Authorities assumed he'd been sleeping or drugged. How else could Annie have snuck up on him? The man would outweigh her by fifty pounds.

While she knew it to be her imagination, the room felt dead. She backed out and closed the door before heading to Annie's room. She used the key card to open the door, then stepped in, closing it behind her.

The room looked as if someone had left in a hurry. Annie had taken most of her things— those Marley had seen at the homeless camp—but a couple of pillows and some clothes still littered the floor.

"Hello, Marley." Gun in hand and aimed at Marley, Annie stepped from the bathroom. "You're the last person I expected to see today."

Marley's heart threatened to beat free of her chest. "Annie. I didn't expect to see you either." She reached behind her for the doorknob.

"Please move forward. If you open that door to run, I will shoot you."

How had she gotten in without the deputy seeing her? "Are you living here again?"

She laughed. "Not in this room. I simply came to gather the rest of my stuff since retrieving the things at the lake won't be easy. Have a seat, please." She waved the gun toward the bed.

"You aren't going to shoot me?" Marley sat slowly and glanced around the room for a weapon. Not finding one, she slid her hand into her bag, ready to press 911.

"Not yet." She leaned against the wall. "But, I will. It'll break my heart. You look so much like my Lauren."

"Your daughter?"

"So, you know about her?" She glowered.

"I heard she was murdered, then you were discharged from the military. I'm very sorry for your loss, but I didn't kill your daughter." Marley felt for the on button on her phone.

"I know that." Annie's face darkened. "Do you think I'm stupid?"

"No, I think you're hurting."

"Having a friend would have healed a lot of my wounds, Marley."

Phone turned on, she moved her fingers around and dialed 911. "What do you plan on doing to me, Annie?"

"You're a reporter. Figure it out. Don't worry. When the time is right, I'll make your death quick. For now, you'll be my safe ride out of town. Now get up. Walk in front of me to your car."

If Annie forced her to drive them out of town,

Marley might never find a way to escape. Outside, her gaze met the startled one of Deputy Johnson who bolted from his car, weapon drawn.

"Drop the gun, Ms. Wilson."

"I don't think so. Me and Marley are going to get in her car and leave this place. If you follow, I'll shoot her." She poked Marley in the back with the gun. "Move."

Marley's gaze locked with the deputy's until she slid into the driver's seat of her car. Annie climbed in the back, apparently to keep the gun aimed at Marley's head.

With a deep, shuddering breath, Marley started the car and backed from the parking space.

~

Dirk's heart dropped to his knees. "What do you mean Annie has Marley?"

"She took her from the motel," the sheriff said. "Deputy Johnson said she must have climbed in a back window because she definitely didn't go past him."

"Any idea where?"

"No. Johnson is following, but he has to stay back enough not to trigger a reaction. They're headed up the mountain. Most likely intending to go down the other side and disappear. The chopper is ready and roadblocks are going up. We'll find them."

"You'd better." Dirk hung up, wishing he had an old-style phone so he could slam down the receiver.

"You okay?" One of the builders glanced over from where he worked on one of the houses.

"No." Dirk stormed away, whistling for Bear to follow. Time to head up the mountain and find her himself. He needed the chance to tell her how much she'd come to mean to him. How much he wanted her to stay in Misty Hollow. Not in a tiny house of her own on some land, but with him on the farm.

~

Annie couldn't believe her luck. Not in an eternity would she have thought that Marley would walk into that motel room.

"Where are we going?"

She met Marley's gaze in the rearview mirror. "I have no idea. Just drive."

"We'll need gas soon. I'm at less than half a tank."

Annie rolled her eyes. "We'll gas up once we're off the mountain. I'm not worried about you running. I've got the gun."

She wished she could've taken care of the farmer, too, for no other reason than he had the friendship Annie craved.

"Did you kill the author?"

"Yes. For the same reason I'm going to kill you. Betrayal."

"I didn't betray you." Marley glanced in the mirror again. "I befriended you when I thought you were Jane, but I can't be friends with a murderer. You kill people, Annie."

"Oh, boo-hoo. There are worse people walking this earth. People who kill children." She glanced out the side window. If she knew who killed Lauren, she'd dismember them. "They never caught the man who killed my child. Maybe if I could find him, I could find closure."

"The police could help."

"Ha. They did nothing."

"I'm sorry for you, I really am, but I cannot allow

this."

Annie's eyes widened as Marley slowed the car's speed, thrust open the car door, and then dove out. She hit the asphalt, then rolled into a ditch.

The car sped to a tree opposite where Marley had landed. Annie covered her eyes, lay on the backseat, and waited for impact.

The next thing she knew, her eyes struggled to open. She didn't know how long she'd been unconscious only that the floorboard of a wrecked vehicle had to be one of the most uncomfortable places. She coughed from the dust the airbags deployed, grabbed the gun from under her, and climbed out one of the back windows.

Every muscle in her body protested. Tiny cuts dotted her arms from the shattered windows.

No games. She'd kill Marley the instant she found her. Her hand tightened on the gun. Anticipation burned through her. Annie could track a deer through thick brush. Tracking a fleeing woman would be easy.

Annie headed to where she'd seen Marley roll before she'd ducked for the crash. A bit of blood dotted the weeds. An injured woman would be even easier to find. Especially if she left a blood trail.

Stupid woman had worn a dress to do her reporting. Pants would've protected her better from scraping the road. If they'd still been friends, Annie could've told her that.

She followed the trail deeper into the forest. It stopped about a hundred feet in. Either the wound had dried, or Marley had found something to bind it with. She studied the area around her.

No rain, so the ground was hard. Dead leaves and

pine needles littered the area providing a cushion against footsteps. But, when Annie got close enough, she'd hear the rustle a foot would make.

The lack of a blood trail was only a minor inconvenience. There. A foot had moved the debris leaving a patch of bare dirt. Annie headed in that direction a lot more slowly than she would've liked. Pain riddled her body from the crash. She cradled her swollen left wrist against her aching side and continued onward.

From the position of the sun, it was late afternoon. Annie had been out for at least a couple of hours. Wonder why no one had found them yet? Then she remembered the mountains were full of remote roads.

Annie glanced up as a helicopter circled. There they were. They'd find the car soon. She forced herself to move faster. In her condition, she wasn't in any shape to get into a fight. She'd be lucky to hit anything if she shot at them. The pain was sharper than anything she'd felt before. Each breath was agony, signifying broken or cracked ribs. She should've worn her seatbelt.

Taking small breaths, she stopped on a game trail next to a creek and searched for signs that Marley had gone that way. Ah, a footprint on the other side of a creek. Smiling, she stepped into the icy cold water and splashed across, soaking her pants to the knee. *Here I come, Marley. Ready or not.*

Chapter Nineteen

The cut on Marley's leg from her tumble into the ditch had stopped bleeding. The road burn on her bare arms reminded her how foolish she'd been to jump. As long as she took it easy, but she needed to increase her speed and find a place to hide. Hopefully, the footprint she'd left before sloshing up the creek would mislead Annie long enough for her to escape.

Tears burned her eyes. She'd acted out of desperation when she'd jumped from the car, not knowing whether she'd survive. But knowing Annie's record for killing, she liked her chances better with the road. Maybe Annie wasn't coming. Maybe she'd died in the crash or was severely injured. Until Marley knew for sure, she wasn't going to let down her guard.

The crazy woman had still been in the car when Marley struggled to her feet, which gave Marley a good head start. It was better to hide until Dirk could find her.

She put a hand to a part of her face that stung. A scrape there, too. She sighed and continued limping along the creek hoping for a hunter's cabin. Heavy clouds had formed overhead, and the last thing she wanted was to be caught in a downpour.

As if she hadn't checked a hundred times, she felt for her cell phone, knowing it was back at the car in her bag. It probably didn't work after the crash, but hopefully, she could still be tracked since she'd left the phone on.

A few sprinkles fell, dotting the leaves at her feet with tiny spots of moisture. Ravenous for a drink, Marley held out her tongue. Not enough to wet her mouth. She should've thought to grab her bag on the way out of the car.

Marley knew she might not make it out of those woods alive. She wouldn't have the chance to finish her book or tell Dirk she loved him. They hadn't had much time for romance, but her heart leaped every time he entered the room or she heard his voice. With Annie out of the picture, she'd hope to explore those feelings.

The tears fell, burning the scrape on her cheek. Keep it together. There's still hope while there's still breath.

The creek ended, flowing underground. Marley's shoulders slumped. No hiding her tracks from a skilled woman like Annie. Eventually, she'd catch up.

The rain fell faster now. Marley limped as fast as she could then tripped over what looked like an overgrown train track, falling hard on her knees. She glanced up and smiled. An abandoned tunnel, covered with vines and almost obscured by bushes loomed in front of her. She'd found a place out of the rain. Marley struggled to her feet, then studied the area around her to see whether she'd left a track. Nothing the rain wouldn't wash away. Picking up a thick stick to lean on, her knees throbbing, she hobbled inside the tunnel. About ten feet inside, she sat in almost complete darkness and kept her gaze trained on the entrance.

The hard rain obscured all sound other than it pounding the packed earth. It also helped hide the tunnel's entrance.

She peered in the opposite direction. What had fallen to shroud the tunnel in darkness?

After resting for a few minutes, she moved through the tunnel, keeping one hand on the wall for guidance. What she found explained why the track had been abandoned.

A rockslide had shut off the entrance except for a small opening at the top. Quite the climb, but she could do it if she had to. She returned to where she could see the dim light from outside. Leaning back against the stone wall, she wrapped her arms around her knees. There wasn't enough light to see how her scrapes were doing or how badly she'd bruised her knees. So, she rested her non-scraped cheek on her knees and dozed from sheer exhaustion.

Any sound that managed to reach her through the heavy rain made her eyes pop open. One of the noises happened to be a rat scurrying through the dried leaves and debris in the tunnel. Marley choked back a shriek and shuddered. As long as the rat left her alone, they'd coexist just fine. She pulled her walking stick closer to her side and leaned her head against the wall behind her.

She'd stay in the tunnel until morning. If no one found her by then, she'd leave and try to find her way down the mountain to town. If Annie came, someone might find Marley's remains next spring before the bushes again covered the entrance.

No, she wouldn't think that way. Marley would survive this to kiss Dirk and tell him she loved him. She'd finish her book and buy a plot of land to build a house on. Maybe she'd get a dog or a cat, or both.

The rain continued past dark. When night fell, so did the temperature. Marley wrapped her arms around her legs and prepared herself for a long, cold night.

~

Annie cursed the rain. She couldn't track a giant in the downpour, and the stupid tree branches above her did nothing to stop her from getting drenched. Now, the temperature had dropped. She'd be an icicle by morning. Annie held her gun under her shirt and tried to keep it dry. The last thing she wanted was a rusty weapon. She glared at the dark sky above her, then hunched her shoulders in an attempt to stay warm. Thank the stars it wasn't wintertime. The only consolation she had was the thought that Marley had to be as miserable as she was.

"Stop!" She screamed at the rain, shivering so hard her teeth started to clatter. "Just stop." She buried her face in lap and rocked.

There was not a time she could remember being this miserable. It was all Marley's fault! If she hadn't run off, Annie wouldn't be in the woods in a downpour.

~

Dirk slammed on the brakes so swiftly at seeing Marley's car smashed into a tree that his truck fishtailed.

Bear whimpered.

"Stay here, boy." Dirk patted the dog's head and grabbed a jacket he kept behind the seat before stepping out into the rain. His headlights lit up the car in front of him.

He pulled the collar of his jacket up, tugged the brim of his cap down, and made a mad dash for the car. The front had been smashed enough that the tree trunk made a V and now stood halfway through the hood. The engine sat in the front seat. Anyone sitting there would have been killed.

The driver's seat sat empty. He tugged on Marley's bag until it pulled free and hooked it over his shoulder. Blood spots stained the back seat. Marley had been driving. So, where was she? Where was Annie?

His heart leaped into his throat as he searched the area around the wrecked vehicle. No sign of either woman. He splashed back to the truck and clipped a leash on Bear's collar.

"We've got some people to find." How badly were they hurt? He fished a flashlight from the glove compartment and donned the backpack he kept in the truck at all times.

As much as he disliked Annie, he didn't want her lying in the woods suffering. The idea that Marley might be lying somewhere made his stomach ache. He glanced in the bag, groaning when he spotted her cell phone. They'd be trying to locate her on foot.

He made sure his jacket covered his weapon to protect it from the rain and headed into the woods, flashlight cutting a faint path as the light tried to get through the rain. The branches broke some of the rainfall but not enough. Water ran off the brim of his hat.

A breeze kicked up, blowing the rain sideways. Fall was coming. Why did it have to show its face when

Marley could be out in it?

It would be hard to find anyone in this hard rain, but he encouraged Bear to find Marley. The dog whined, then nose to the ground, led Dirk deeper into the forest.

He shivered as rain ran down a tree branch and past the collar of his jacket. It wouldn't take long for his jacket to become drenched. Mud already caked his shoes making his steps heavier.

Bear stopped at an overflowing creek. Crossing would not be safe.

Dirk glanced up and down the creek. If Bear thought Marley had crossed, then they would have to. He went up creek to where several low-lying branches might provide handholds. He'd tie Bear's leash around his arm so the dog didn't get swept away and cross hand over hand using the branches. It would work. It had to.

"Well, hope this works." Dirk glanced at the dog, shoved the flashlight inside his jacket, then grabbed the first branch.

He made it to the second branch and closed his hand around it before being yanked off his feet. The water had swept Bear to the length of his leash and pulled Dirk along with him.

He reached out for anything he could find to hold onto. Dirk didn't know how far the creek went, or if it went underground at some point. All he knew was that he did not want to find out.

Bracing his feet, he tried to catch them on a boulder under the water. The whites of Bear's eyes let Dirk know how frightened the dog was. "Hang on, boy."

He finally got his feet under him and fought against the rushing water to reach the other side. When he did, reeling Bear in like a big fish, he collapsed on the bank to catch his breath. Hopefully, if Marley had come this way, it had been before the creek flooded. The idea of finding her body washed up somewhere was more than he could deal with.

Breath back to normal and thoroughly soaked, Dirk stood. "Find Marley."

After running in circles for several minutes, the dog sat and stared up at Dirk.

Great. They'd lost the trail.

No longer caring about stealth, he cupped his hands around his mouth. "Marley!" Could anyone even hear over the rain? "Marley!"

When no answer came, he chose to go upstream. His feet squished in his shoes, his toes growing numb from the cold. The wind had died a bit, but being thoroughly soaked kept him chilled. Unless he found shelter; he couldn't build a fire.

Bear trudged at his side, head down, looking as miserable as Dirk felt. "Sorry, boy. I'll make it up to you when we get home. I have a steak in the freezer."

The dog's ears perked up a bit at the mention of steak.

Dirk shoved his hands in his pockets, peered up from under the brim of his dripping hat, hunched his shoulders, and pushed on. Misty Mountain was a huge place. With the storm, the helicopter couldn't lift off. The sheriff had told Dirk he wouldn't have help from the sky until the storm lifted, but volunteers would be searching on foot.

Occasionally, he'd stop and give a futile call of her

name, praying for a response. The further he went, the more discouraged he became.

They came to the end of the creek with no sign of Marley. Dirk took a deep, shuddering breath but refused to give up hope completely. No sign might be a good sign, right? It was much better than finding her severely wounded or dead. Unless he found a body, he wouldn't stop searching.

The light started to dim on his flashlight. He slapped it against his palm. The beam brightened. The creek had beaten it up a bit. If they lost the light it gave them, they'd have to wait until morning and suffer through the night without shelter.

Chapter Twenty

Something wet and cold pressed against Marley's cheek. She opened her eyes. "Bear?" The dog licked her face.

"Thank God." Dirk rushed into the tunnel and knelt beside her, running his hands up and down her arms. "Are you okay?"

"I'm freezing." Water dripped from him. "You don't look much better."

"No, I'm not. Now that we're under a roof, of sorts, I can start a fire." He handed Marley her bag.

"Thank you." She grabbed the water bottle from inside and guzzled half of it down before handing it back to him. "You can refill it at the waterfall if you want to before you start the fire. I'll look for anything that will burn in this tunnel."

"Sounds like a plan." He finished the water and exited the tunnel, leaving Bear with her.

Everything would be fine now. Dirk was with her. She retrieved her phone from her bag, grateful it still worked other than the fact she had no service and used it as a flashlight as she gathered sticks and dry leaves from inside the tunnel. It wouldn't make a lasting fire, but it might be enough to dry and warm them. Even a little while would make a huge difference. Of course, she did have her notebook. It had plenty of blank pages.

"Full bottle." Dirk set the bottle on the ground and nodded at the pile of stuff to burn. "Good job." He pulled a lighter from his pocket and, using a sheet of paper from her notebook, he started a flame.

Other than his face, Marley hadn't seen anything better in a long time. She gave a long sigh as the warmth permeated her hands.

Dirk shed his jacket and laid it near the fire. "I'm going to shine my flashlight on you now. I need to see where you're injured."

"It's nothing but scrapes."

"Nope, that cut on your leg doesn't look good. How'd you do that?" He smoothed her hair away from her face, revealing the scrape on her cheek. "Or this?"

"I jumped out of the car while it was still going and rolled into a ditch." She gave a sheepish smile. "It's the only thing I could think of. It worked." She shrugged.

His mouth fell open, then he snapped it shut. "You jumped from a moving vehicle?"

"Yep. I haven't seen any sign of Annie, so she must not have made it out." She shuddered, even though the fire's warmth was starting to seep into her bones.

"I found the car, and she wasn't in it. I've not seen any signs of her, either."

"Do you think she's gone? Gave up?"

Dirk shook his head and ripped off one of his sleeves. He poured some water on the makeshift rag and dabbed the cut on her leg before tying the sleeve around the wound. "She isn't the type to give up. Nothing will stop her but death or prison."

She hissed against the pain of him tightening the bandage. "Well, I'd hoped. At least you found me and not her. I'm sure she'll be very angry at this point." If, in fact, she stilled lived. Once Dirk's ministrations were complete—he'd even cleaned the scrape on her face—she stepped closer to the fire.

"I'm going to fill this bottle again, then get dry. We'll be fine for a while if we ration water." He ducked back outside.

While he was gone, she fished a protein bar from her bag and tore it in half. Who knew how long the rain would last? At least they had a roof over their heads and water.

"This is all I have." She handed him half when he returned.

"I've got a couple of water bottles and a box of granola bars. Some treats for Bear." He jerked his thumb toward the backpack he'd set against the wall. "I keep it stocked for such a time as this. We'll be fine if the rain doesn't last too long. If it doesn't stop by morning, I say we hike out anyway. I doubt the sticks will last that long anyway."

She was tempted to suggest they head out that day, but the heavy deluge dissuaded her. Maybe by morning, it would have stopped or slowed to a drizzle. "Do you have service on your phone?"

"Nope. Otherwise, I'd have called the sheriff when I found the car. He said there might be volunteers braving the weather to search, but I doubt it. If it wasn't you out here, I'm not sure I would have."

"Yes, you would." She ginned. "That's the type of person you are. Kind, brave…" As beautiful inside as out.

"Yeah, I most likely would." His grin matched hers. "But especially since it's you."

She warmed more from his words and the look in his eyes than the fire. "I'm very glad you did."

They sat around the fire and told each other how they found the cave. Her heart skipped a beat to hear of him crossing a swollen creek with the dog. "You could both have drowned." She might never have found him. "How would I go on without you?"

"Hold onto that thought. There's something I want to discuss with you when we get out of here." His voice grew husky.

"I've something to say myself." She almost told him right then that she loved him but bit off the words when Bear lunged to his feet, gaze fixed on the tunnel entrance.

A very wet Annie burst into their shelter. She stopped immediately, her eyes wide and bright. "Well, well, well. I did not expect to find you guys here all warm and cozy." She gestured a gun at them. "By the wall. It's my turn by the fire. If your dog attacks, I will shoot him."

"Come, Bear." Dirk kept himself between her and Marley.

She put her hands on his back until she reached the tunnel wall. Nothing about this scenario led her to believe it would end well.

~

What a pleasant surprise. Just when Annie had given up on finding Marley—thinking her dead in the woods somewhere—she stumbled upon her and the farmer. Once her fingers were warm enough to pull the trigger, she'd complete her mission and leave this godforsaken place.

The warmth of the fire slowly chased away the chill that had been on her for hours. Feeling returned to her fingers.

She'd been so wrapped up in getting warm and relishing the fact she'd soon be rid of both of them that she didn't see the farmer reach into a backpack until it was too late.

His bullet struck her.

Her finger twitched, firing her weapon as she fell.

The last thing she saw was Lauren's face bending over her. "I just wanted to be your friend," she said softly. A tear slid down her cheek as darkness took her.

~

"Get away from her." Dirk hissed against the fire in his side. He felt for an exit wound. Great. The bullet was lodged inside him.

"Oh, you've been hit." She rushed to his side.

"Find something to tie around me. I'll be fine." He forced the words through his teeth.

A few minutes later, she returned with a scarf that had been wrapped around Annie's neck. "I hate using something of hers, but there isn't anything else." She tied it as tight around him as she could. "Anything else?"

"We can't stay here any longer." Dirk didn't want to say so, but his blood was already soaking the scarf. He refused to die in the tunnel with Annie's body nearby. "I need to make sure she's dead."

"She is. There's no pulse. You got her in the chest,

Dirk. I'm worried about *you* now."

So, was he. "Help me up."

She propped her shoulder under his, almost buckling under his weight. "I'd give you my walking stick, but we burned it. Are you sure we have to leave?"

"Yes. I need to find somewhere with cell reception."

"You're hurt bad." It wasn't a question.

"Afraid so, sweetheart." Leaning on her, they left the tunnel back into the rain which had, thankfully, slowed to a drizzle. They'd still be wet, but at least they could see. "We can't go back the way I came. I'll never make it across the creek."

"Should we follow it as far down as it will go? Is that the direction of the road?"

"Yes, but it'll be a long walk." He lifted his voice. "Find truck, Bear." He'd managed to find Marley in a downpour; surely his nose could find the truck. Dirk only hoped it would be before he succumbed to his injury.

He wasn't sure how long they walked before he had to stop. He leaned against a tree and prayed for enough strength to make it to the truck. After a few minutes, he pushed away.

"Here." Marley handed him a thick stick with a V on the end. "I can't hold you anymore." Tears shimmered in her eyes. "This is one time being petite is not a good thing."

"This is perfect." Using the makeshift crutch for support, he followed her and his dog down the mountain.

The stick would lodge in the mud on occasion; he'd almost fallen forward when the incline became steep, but foot by foot, they made some progress.

"Mason!"

He glanced up to see the sheriff and Deputy Johnson rushing their way. "We found your truck and the wrecked car. Man, am I glad to see the two of you." His eyes narrowed. "You're injured."

"Annie. Her body is in an abandoned train tunnel. The one that suffered a rockslide ten years ago."

The sheriff sent Johnson to check her out. "I'll call for medical. The road isn't far. The helicopter spotted the vehicles about twenty minutes ago. It went airborne as soon as the rain slowed enough for him to see."

He let Dirk lean on him. "The two of you look like you've been living in the woods for months. No offense."

"None taken." Dirk chuckled, then groaned. Laughing, breathing, walking, all sent shards of glass through his side. His gaze fell on Marley. He'd do it all again if it meant rescuing her.

With both her and the sheriff helping him, he made it to the road without passing out. They helped him inside the truck, then Marley climbed into the passenger side. Now, they waited.

She reached across and took his hand. "You okay?"

"Still breathing." Blood had soaked through the scarf and now soaked the waistband of his jeans.

"Make sure you stay that way. I meant it when I said I don't know what I'd do without you, Dirk. I love you. You're the reason I want to put down roots in Misty Hollow."

"I wanted to say it first."

"Say what?" She smiled.

He brought her hand to his lips. "That I love you. I don't want you living in a tiny house somewhere away from me. Move to the farm. Let's see whether romance between us will happen."

"Oh, it'll happen." She arched a brow. "Do you have enough strength to kiss me?"

"I think *you* should kiss me." Before he passed out, preferably, because at that moment, he could only see her through a tunnel.

As her lips pressed against his, his eyes drifted closed. No matter how many times she called his name, he couldn't respond. Then, complete darkness overtook him.

~

When he woke up, he found himself in a hospital bed. Marley, fresh bandages on her knees and leg, slept curled up in a chair. He groaned and raised the bed to a sitting position.

Her eyes popped open, and she moved to his side. "You scared me."

"I'm sorry. How long have I been out?"

"Two days. They did surgery as soon as they got you prepped after the ambulance brought us here. Deputy Johnson brought your truck and took Bear home." She cupped his face. "They extracted the bullet. You're going to make a full recovery, but you needed a blood transfusion." She smiled. "I was a good match. My blood now flows through your veins, just like you are in my heart." She planted a gentle kiss on his lips.

"Hmm. When can I get out of here?"

"Tomorrow, maybe." She straightened. "I'll go let the nurse know you're awake."

She left the room. He glanced at the window. A

sunshine-filled day in more ways than one. He'd gone under on a dismal day and awoke to a bright one. A day as bright as he hoped their future would be.

164

Epilogue

Even after six months, Marley couldn't forget the tear that slid down Annie's cheek as she whispered the words, "I just wanted to be your friend." Her heart ached for the woman's madness and loneliness. More than once, she'd shed tears of her own.

That day could have ended so much worse. She smiled as Dirk exited the house. Married three months, and it still felt like a dream.

He took her hand and pulled her to her feet before kissing her. "Ready?"

"Absolutely." The last of the tiny-house residents moved in that morning and they wanted to welcome their new neighbor, Willy, who had finally decided to leave his tent for a roof over his head after a few chilly nights.

The man sat outside his tiny house, cigarette dangling from his lips, and waved. "All settled in. Not that I had much." He gave a raspy laugh. "You healed up?"

"Yep." Dirk grinned. "Except for a scar to impress the ladies with, I'm all good."

Marley gave him a playful punch in his upper arm. "The only lady you need to impress, mister, is me."

"I heard there's some good news," Willy said.

She smiled up at Dirk. "More than one thing. My book is going to be published, and we're having a baby."

"We are?" Dirk's mouth fell open. "Really?"

"Really." She cupped his cheek. "Come springtime, you're going to be a daddy."

His eyes shimmered, and he wrapped her in a hug. "Wow."

Willy hobbled to his feet. "I know this is my little piece of land, but I'll go inside and give the two of you some privacy."

Marley laughed and stepped back. "Like all the other residents aren't standing outside watching." Maybe she should've waited to tell Dirk that piece of news, but she hadn't been able to contain herself.

He took her hand and led her toward the renovated barn. "Come and see. The studio is finished. I have enlisted three women from town for their first lesson tomorrow." Taking a deep breath, he slid the doors open. Marley hadn't been allowed inside for weeks. Dirk had wanted to keep the place a surprise until completed.

"Wow." Wrestling mats were piled in a corner. A wall of mirrors made the place more cavernous than before. Stalls had morphed into changing rooms and showers. "You added exercise equipment?"

"Sure. Why not let people have a gym membership? We don't have a gym in Misty Hollow. This way, they won't have to drive to Langley." He put his arm around her waist.

She laid her head on his shoulder. "It looks wonderful, Dirk."

Their future shone like the sun. Her life was fuller than she'd ever dreamed it could be.

Thank you, Annie, for sending me to Misty Hollow.

The End

www.cynthiahickey.com

Cynthia Hickey is a multi-published and best-selling author of cozy mysteries and romantic suspense. She has taught writing at many conferences and small writing retreats. She and her husband run the publishing press, Winged Publications, which includes some of the CBA's best well-known authors. They live in Arizona and Arkansas, becoming snowbirds with three dogs. They have ten grandchildren who keep them busy and tell everyone they know that "Nana is a writer."

Don't miss the other books in the Misty Hollow series:

Shop my bookstore
Connect with me on FaceBook
Twitter
Sign up for my newsletter and receive a free short story
www.cynthiahickey.com

Follow me on Amazon
And Bookbub
Shop my bookstore here. For better price and autographed.

Enjoy other books by Cynthia Hickey

Misty Hollow
Secrets of Misty Hollow
Deceptive Peace
Calm Surface
Lightning Never Strikes Twice
Lethal Inheritance
Bitter Isolation
Say I Don't
Christmas Stalker

9 781959 788812